Wynter wasn't the kind of girl a man could do casual with. Even if she wasn't the boss's daughter.

I might as well walk into a wall.

"Tell me something Wynter Worthington," I said.

Her lips curved into a half smile.

"Tell you what Cooper?"

My name on her lips held promises she didn't even realize she was making.

"Does your daddy bring all his new hires home on the first day?"

She shrugged, sweeping her hair back and letting it fall over her left shoulder.

"When it suits him," she said, looking up at me from beneath lowered lashes.

I straightened on the stool. Leaned back. It occurred to me that this girl was flirting with me.

I was an expert in the flirting department.

And she was definitely flirting.

I looked over my shoulder, at what, I couldn't say. Maybe looked to see if Noah was walking through the door.

I hadn't calculated this into my plan.

"You shouldn't be doing that," I said.

She was going to get me in trouble.

"Doing what?" she asked innocently, with an exaggerated southern drawl.

"You know what," I said, with a shake of my head. Then I looked away. Looking into her eyes was like looking into trouble.

She stuck the tines of her fork into her pie crust and put a tiny flake of that crust into her mouth.

She was danger and I couldn't look away.

"I should probably go," I said.

She tapped the screen of her phone, bringing up a text I couldn't read from here.

"You can if you want to," she said. "But Daddy's going to be back in an hour."

"What does he want?" I asked, certain that she knew.

"I wouldn't know," she said.

"Well," I said, standing up. "He can give me a call. We can reschedule." I turned around. "Thanks for the pie," I said, over my shoulder.

Whatever Noah wanted couldn't possibly be worth getting into trouble with his daughter.

THREE BROKEN RULES

THREE BROKEN RULES

THE WORTHINGTONS

KATHRYN KALEIGH

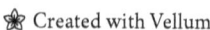

To learn more about Kathryn Kaleigh, visit

www.kathrynkaleigh.com

Kathryn Kaleigh

1

WYNTER WORTHINGTON

I slid my reading glasses off my nose to the top of my head and looked out the little oval window of the Lear jet taking me home.

As I took the air pods out of my ears, one, then the other, the familiar roar of the jet replaced the soft background music I'd been listening to.

My job took me all over the country. But each and every time I returned to Houston, I got butterflies in my stomach.

They were good butterflies, usually.

Born and bred in Houston, no matter where I traveled, Houston had my heart. It was home.

It was a warm cloudless May morning and even though the plane wasn't even on the ground yet, the air felt different than up north. Softer.

It made no sense, but when I could see the tops of the trees, I felt like I was practically on the ground.

I wasn't a nervous flyer, but only because I couldn't afford to be.

I was the youngest of the four daughters of Noah and Savannah Worthington.

THE Noah Worthington of Skye Travels.

I had earlier memories of flying in airplanes than I did of riding in automobiles.

But that was just the way the mind worked.

Memories were a funny thing.

Not always accurate, but quite powerful.

It didn't take much to send me down a rabbit hole when it came to thinking about thinking.

I'd done my dissertation on metacognition. And it had paid off enormously. I was one of the most sought after consultants in my field—industrial/organizational psychology.

I gathered up my wire-bound notebook and pencil and shoved them into my leather bookbag.

I liked to use the quiet flying time to brainstorm or just to think.

Momma would call it meditation. And it was. When I wanted to get technical, I called flying a positive addiction.

All the pilots in my family agreed with me. And we certainly had enough of them. Pilots in the family. Five to be exact.

That was a lot of pilots in one family.

I had nothing against pilots, specifically. But I had a lot of insights into their way of life. And I'd argue with anyone who said their way of life wasn't different.

And, yes, I would admit that my daddy was an exception. And my sister, Ainsley. Probably. She was older than me, though, and I couldn't say what she'd done before she met her husband, Wyatt.

And, Momma was Daddy's second wife. So for all I knew, Daddy had gone through a cad stage, too.

As much as I loved Daddy, it didn't change my opinion of the pilot lifestyle.

"Prepare for landing," Jackson said over the speaker.

Jackson was my sister Brianna's fiancé. A good pilot. More

often than not, Daddy assigned him to my flight, either Jackson or Daddy flew me himself.

Personally, I didn't make any specific requests about pilots. I knew that as long as I was flying with Skye Travels, I was in good hands.

Daddy only hired the best in the field.

If something was going to happen on a flight, it was just going to happen.

I checked my seatbelt. I hadn't even bothered to unhook it on the flight from Chicago to Houston.

The airplane rocked gently as we passed over the top of the suburban mall just before Jackson took it in for a smooth, as always, landing.

It wasn't that there was anything wrong with pilots.

I liked them just fine.

It was their lifestyle. The uniform. The glamour of travel. The mystique.

As we taxied along the runway, I saw that my car was already there. Ready to take me to my parents' house.

Sure. It was uncommon for a twenty-five-year-old professional to live with her parents, but it saved me tons of money.

I'd commuted to the University of Houston and now I spent probably seventy-five percent of my time on the road.

It would make no sense to pay for a place of my own when I was never there.

As I waited for Jackson to secure the plane, I stared out the window.

The red Skye Travels logo was emblazoned across the building's new glass door.

The driver of my car came through that door and walked outside onto the tarmac.

I hadn't seen this driver before, but although I knew most

of the drivers, I didn't know all of them. I didn't know all the pilots either for that matter.

The driver was wearing black pants and a solid white button-down shirt with a solid black tie. No jacket and no cap.

He had short dark hair and, even though he wore black sunshades, I could see that he wasn't a day over thirty.

His walk caught my attention. He actually walked with the familiar swagger of a pilot.

Stopping at the car, the usual black SUV, he looked in my direction.

My heart did a little flip and I noted a strong physical attraction to him. Stronger than usual.

I looked away. Checked my phone messages.

As a frequent traveler myself, I didn't date in my own back yard.

Perhaps being a frequent traveler myself was the very reason I knew so much about their lifestyle.

I lived it myself.

So that was how I came around to my first rule of dating.

Never crush on a pilot.

2

COOPER ABRAMS

*I*t was one of those clear, cloudless Texas mornings that smelled hot. It may be just the end of May, but I'd lived in Houston long enough to know that it didn't matter.

It was full on summer.

I'd left my jacket inside the office in the private terminal and as I stood with the sun beating down on the top of my head, I decided to hell with it and rolled up my shirt sleeves.

It was my first day on the job and my task for the day was to pick up the boss's daughter from someone else's flight and drive her home.

So much for thinking that I was going to start off this job doing what I loved most.

Flying.

I'd watched the pilot of the Lear jet make a smooth as silk landing then taxi over to the private terminal of Skye Travels.

Breathing in the heady scent of jet fuel, I stood next to the shiny black sedan.

The driver was in the restroom upstairs puking his guts out.

I was only in this situation because I'd had compassion for the guy.

The receptionist had been right in the middle of ordering my uniforms when we'd heard the guy in the bathroom. And, of course, I'd volunteered to check on him.

The poor guy had been distraught that he wouldn't be there to pick up someone named Wynter.

I'd done my homework on Skye Travels and in the process I'd learned that about half of the Worthington family was involved in this particular aviation business, many of them pilots.

It didn't bother me. I knew it was a family run business. That's how it worked.

What did bother me was that somehow I'd missed knowing that there was a fourth daughter named Wynter.

Apparently, she somehow managed to keep a low profile.

I adjusted my tie as the pilot opened the door. I was a hair's breath away from just loosening it. Since I wasn't flying, there didn't seem to be much point in wearing the tie while I stood out in the heat.

But before I could loosen my tie, a young lady stepped out of the plane. She was a thousand times different from what I was expecting, though if someone had asked me what I was expecting, I wouldn't have had an answer for them.

I wasn't sure if I'd been expecting a hot party girl or a younger version of Mrs. Worthington—pretty, but serious. Part of that expectation came from the driver's obvious loyalty.

This girl was neither of those.

She was dressed all in black. A black pencil skirt and a matching short jacket over a black blouse.

Before going down the steps in her black high heels, she pulled a pair of black sunshades out of her bag and put them over her eyes.

Damn. I'd gotten no more than a glimpse, but from that simple glimpse, I saw that she was stunningly beautiful.

I'd seen pictures of her sisters and had been impressed by how pretty they all were. Noah's wife, too.

But even that didn't prepare me for this petite elfin girl with straight shoulder-length hair.

I usually went for the girls with long hair, so it was especially surprising that I felt that immediate gut kick of attraction to someone who wasn't my usual type.

The warm Texas wind blew her hair into her face and she pushed it impatiently away before putting one hand on the rail and starting to make her way down the steps.

She moved with a combination of caution and grace.

It occurred to me that this might not even be Wynter.

But when the pilot followed her down the steps, I knew it had to be her.

"I'll get your bags," the pilot said.

"Thank you, Jackson," she said. Her voice carried a slight huskiness to it that made her even more attractive.

As she came toward the Land Rover, I remembered that I was her driver.

The key was in the car and it was already running, so I opened the back door and stepped aside for her to climb inside.

"Thank you," she said with a little smile.

I wanted to see more of that smile, but without the sunshades hiding her eyes.

After closing the door behind her, I opened the trunk and helped Jackson load two suitcases.

"Take care of her," Jackson said, with a clap on my shoulder.

"Sure thing," I said. "Nice landing."

"Thanks," Jackson said. "See 'ya around." Then he turned and went inside.

He didn't know who I was. Didn't know that I was the newest Skye Travels pilot.

He didn't know. And neither did Wynter.

I climbed into the driver's seat and looked into the rearview mirror.

"Where can I take you, Miss Worthington?" I asked.

3

WYNTER

I settled into the back seat of the SUV and took off my sunglasses. The air conditioning was blowing at full force, keeping the oncoming outside heat at bay.

"Home please," I said, looking into the driver's eyes in the rearview mirror.

I sensed an air of patience about him.

He nodded once and tapped the GPS screen.

"Can I get the address?" he asked, then looked at me in the mirror. "just to confirm."

I rattled off my address and he tapped a line on the screen.

"You're new," I said, turning the vent off my face.

He grinned, looking at me again in the mirror.

"It's actually my first day," he said.

"Oh," I said. "Well. I hope it's going well."

He drove the car around the plane and took off toward the gate. I pulled my phone out and checked it, mostly out of boredom.

"It's nothing like I expected," he said.

I set my phone down.

"How is it different?" I asked, finding the conversation much more interesting than scrolling through my messages.

He pulled out onto the freeway.

"I didn't expect to be driving, for one thing," he said.

"You thought you'd be shadowing," I said.

"Something like that," he said as he switched lanes.

The traffic was light right now. I estimated he'd have me home in about fifteen minutes.

"I didn't catch your name," I said, scooting over toward the middle of the bench seat, but the seatbelt had me locked in place.

"Cooper," he said.

And obviously Cooper was a man of few words.

"It's nice to meet you Cooper," I said, determined to get him talking. "Where are you from?"

"Originally Alabama," he said.

I smiled. "My mother is from Alabama."

"Small world," he said, holding the steering wheel loosely.

"How did you end up in Houston?"

He didn't answer at first. Seemed distracted by the GPS.

I could see why he didn't expect to drive today. He seemed unfamiliar with both the car and the roads.

He took the correct exit and headed toward Memorial Drive.

"Work," he said, looking back at me with an odd expression.

"What?" I asked, teasingly. "There's no need for drivers in Alabama?"

"I thought I'd like a change of scenery," he said.

I looked out the window as we drove though one of the most upscale residential areas of Houston.

I'd visited my grandmother in Alabama. She still lived in a modest, but comfortable house in a quiet neighborhood. Too quiet for my taste.

"Do you find it to be much different here?" I asked.

Cooper, too, looked around. "I'll let you know," he said, turning right at the stop sign.

A few minutes later we pulled up to my parents' house. It was unassuming, modest looking from the outside.

But on the other side of the front there was a house big enough to get lost in. There was a courtyard, for God's sake. Momma had said the courtyard was the selling point for her. Said it reminded her of a castle.

It had to be big to raise a family of five. And at least half the time, one of us had a friend over. Then there was the housekeeper and the nanny.

It was much quieter now that I was the only one of their children living at home.

I never heard either Momma or Daddy complain about me living there. To be honest, the way our busy schedules were, I rarely saw them.

Cooper put the car in park.

"Big place for a little girl," he said.

It took me a second to realize he didn't know that this was my parents' house. I wasn't offended by his statement in the least. Something about the way he said it actually sounded like a compliment.

"I like a lot of space," I said, putting my phone back in my handbag and unhooking my seatbelt.

"I'll get the door," he said, getting out of the car and stepping back to open my door.

With one hand on the door, he held out his other hand for me.

I put my hand in his to allow him to help me step out of the car. Anyone who said it was possible to get out of an SUV gracefully while wearing a straight skirt and heels was lying.

I found not being able to see Cooper's eyes behind his dark shades a little bit disconcerting, but mostly disappointing.

I wanted to see his eyes. To see if he was handsome with his shades off as he was with them on.

He closed the door behind me and tucked my hand in the crook of his arm.

It was a surprisingly old-fashioned move that caught me off guard.

I didn't tell him, but I thought that Cooper was going to do just fine as a driver. Or whatever else he decided to do for that matter.

He led me to the front door and released my hand.

"I'll wait for you to get inside," he said.

Instead of opening the door, I just looked at him. I appreciated him escorting me to the door and seeing me safely inside, but...

"Is there something else I can do?" he asked.

I lifted a brow.

"I'm going to need my luggage," I said.

My sense was that Cooper rarely forgot anything and even more, was rarely flustered.

But today was the exception.

4

COOPER

I trained the GPS back to the Skye Travels office and drove through the old neighborhood, canopied with large oak trees that muted some of the sun's heat.

I should have told Wynter who I was.

That I wasn't her driver, but instead was one of her father's pilots.

But I'd been enjoying getting to know her in another capacity.

She didn't know I worked for her father, so she'd had no reason to be anything other than herself.

I wouldn't have minded having more time to get to know her, but the trip went by quickly.

I didn't find it odd to have a conversation with her sitting behind me. I did that all the time.

Actually, oddly enough, being a pilot was a lot like being a taxi driver.

It was just so much more fun to travel over the top of everything than it was to have to navigate traffic.

Like most pilots, I didn't care for how long it took to get from one place to another on the ground.

Today was the exception.

I was sitting at a light when I got a message from my new boss.

NOAH: *Are you still at my house?*

My house?

Why did my boss think I was at his house?

ME: *Just dropped Wynter off at her house*

The light turned green and just as I was starting to move again, another message came in.

NOAH: *I'm headed that way now. Meet me there and we can go over some things.*

Now I was totally confused.

ME: *At her house?*

The traffic was moving so I didn't have time to ask anything further.

I did, however, get a response back.

Noah sent me Wynter's address. The address I'd just left.

Dammit.

I made a U-turn at the next intersection.

That could only mean one thing.

Wynter still lived with her parents.

Not that I cared. Or that it was any of my business.

But I was about to show up back up at her house—their house—and she was going to find out that I wasn't who she thought I was.

Not that it mattered.

Except that it did matter to me.

I'd just dropped her off… as her driver… and forgot to get her luggage out of the back.

I didn't normally get flustered around women.

Wynter was the exception.

I also kept my attention off of women where I worked. I certainly never let myself have an attraction to the boss's daughter.

Wynter was the exception.

5

WYNTER

*O*ne of the things I liked best about my room was the view.

I had set up a little home office area in what was essentially a glassed-in balcony. It had glass on three sides and on one side I could look out over my MacBook Pro at the street outside the front of the house. My other view was the lawn at the side of the house.

There was an old mimosa tree outside my window that I'd watched grow over the years.

Right now in May, delicate pink flowers were everywhere, their blossoms spilling out of the tree onto the ground. I honestly didn't know if pink was my favorite color because of this tree or if this was my favorite tree because pink was my favorite color.

There was a thick limb, curved just right into a seat, a few feet up where I used to spend reading on some of the few days when the weather was temperate.

It was calm, peaceful. And I had a lot of fond memories growing up here.

I opened up my computer and logged into my email.

There was one email inquiring about my services.

It was from a company based out of Los Angeles. They were a small start-up company.

I copied and pasted my standard response to inquiries. Changed a few words to tailor the email to them and sent it right back.

That was one thing people liked about me. I didn't put things off.

As the whoosh of the outgoing email faded, a black SUV turned into the circle driveway.

I watched as it slowly came to a stop.

It looked exactly like the car Cooper had driven me home in. But he would have no reason to come back here.

Then Daddy, driving his black Dodge pickup truck, pulled up followed by familiar sound of the garage door opening. I hadn't seen Daddy in four days.

I closed my computer, but instead of standing up, I took another look at the black SUV sitting in the circle drive.

The driver's door opened and Cooper stepped out.

Why was he here?

I hadn't left anything in the car. He'd forgotten my luggage, but I reminded him.

It was his first day on the job so I didn't fault him for it. Besides, he'd been really sweet helping me to the door.

Whatever his reason for being back was, I was sure it had nothing to do with me.

Maybe Daddy had called for a car.

Sometimes he did that when he needed someone to drive while he sat in the back seat and made phone calls or did other business.

And even though it certainly had nothing to do with me, seeing him again had my blood racing.

He was a handsome man. Lean and tall, but not too tall. Perfect really.

He took a minute to unroll his sleeves and button them at the cuff before he headed to the door.

For the second time, I noticed that he walked with the confidence I usually saw in the pilots who worked for Daddy.

As he rang the doorbell, his image appeared on my phone.

I picked it up and watched him.

After he slid his dark glasses off and tucked one stem into his shirt, he unknowingly looked right into the camera.

I sucked in my breath. I'd thought he was handsome before, but now, seeing him without the dark shades, I saw that he was just as hot as I'd imagined. Maybe more.

This was not good.

I was crushing on the chauffeur. And not just any chauffeur. The one who worked for Daddy.

6

COOPER

*T*he housekeeper opened the door. She was a woman in her thirties. Pretty. Friendly.

The only way I knew she was the housekeeper was her uniform.

Apparently the Worthington family liked their employees to wear black.

I stepped inside out of the heat into a wide foyer and the noisy road outside muted in a barely noticeable background roar. Besides being pleasantly cool, it smelled like cinnamon and vanilla. But definitely a strong scent of cinnamon. Like someone was baking a pie.

The floors were light oak wood with not a speck of dust.

To my right was a wide staircase leading upstairs. To my left was a tall grandfather clock, steadily ticking away the minutes.

There were archways to the right and the left. And straight ahead were massive French doors leading out into a courtyard with a little fountain and a bench.

A solid white cat with a black streak across its face and a black tail sat on that bench, diligently washing one of its paws.

"Mr. Worthington just texted," the housekeeper said. "He'll be here in a second if you'd like to wait here."

"Sure," I said, going to stand at the glass doors overlooking the courtyard.

A butterfly swooped down, getting the cat's attention.

Although the butterfly was living dangerously, the cat gave it a cursory glance and went back to washing.

Noah's house reminded me of a castle.

A castle in the middle of Houston.

The courtyard was surrounded by two-story walls, about half having windows.

Had Wynter grown up here with her four siblings? I couldn't help but wonder what that must have been like.

Wondered if she had had a fairytale childhood or if it just looked that way on the surface.

I heard Noah walking toward me before I saw him. He was talking on the phone. He stopped when he saw me and motioned for me to follow him.

Talking to someone about upgrading a computer program, Noah led me around a corner into a wide-open space that was obviously his home office.

At first I thought his office took up one side of the whole house. But as I sat in one of two big comfortable chairs in front of the window, I realized that Noah had only half the area.

The other area obviously belonged to someone else.

Where Noah had little model airplanes around his part of the office, the other part did not. Instead there were photographs of the family scattered around and a potted tree.

The colors were the same. All a mix of light and dark gray.

The other office no doubt belonged to Dr. Savannah Worthington, a well-known psychologist in her field. I knew because I'd run across her name while I was researching the company.

I wondered how a pilot and psychologist got along. What

would they talk about? From what everyone said, Noah and Savannah had a strong marriage. And five children. So maybe talking wasn't their strong suit. Whatever it was worked just fine for them.

Noah ended his call and sat down in the chair next to mine.

"Thanks for driving my daughter home," he said.

"No need to thank me," I said. "I'm happy to be part of the team."

Noah smiled and shook his head a little at the cliché. I was going to have to do better than tossing out overused statements like that.

And I would never tell Noah how disappointed I'd been to have my first assignment be driving a car instead of flying an airplane

And I would never ever tell him that I would have happily done far more than just drive his daughter home.

I changed into a pair of blue jeans and a long-sleeve t-shirt. I always wore long sleeve t-shirts inside because Daddy kept the house cold in summer.

I didn't complain. I preferred cold weather myself over the scorching heat of south Texas.

As I ran a brush through my shorter than normal hair, I realized my hands were trembling.

That was from crushing on Cooper.

I'd planned on taking a nap. Using the rest of the day to recoup after a long week of work. My pattern was to work long days, sometimes into the night. Then I'd come home. Take some time. Rest.

It worked well for me. Momma had been a drug rep when she was my age. She cautioned me that rest was crucial. I don't think she took time to rest, so she should know.

But my curiosity wasn't going to let me relax my mind. I knew it as certain as I knew I was going to take the next breath.

I put on a pair of white canvas sneakers and headed into the hallway.

I paused long enough to watch our little black and white cat bat at a butterfly while her brother, a big orange cat, stretched out on the stone wall of the fountain and closed his eyes.

I sighed. I loved my work. But sometimes I missed just being at home.

Fortunately, I had three days before I had to leave for my next job.

And right now those three whole days stretched out in front of me like an oasis, even though I knew the time would fly by.

As I reached the bottom of the stairs, I heard Daddy's voice coming from his office. Not a surprise that he had Cooper in his office.

Since it wouldn't be appropriate for me to just barge in on them, I turned right instead and went into the kitchen for a bottle of cold water.

The housekeeper, Elise, was pulling a pie out of the oven. I swear I think Elise sometimes cooked pies so the house would smell good. Momma would take a bite at most and Daddy wasn't supposed to eat sweets, but we all knew he did.

Elise probably secretly made the pies for Daddy.

"How was your trip?" Elise asked.

I opened the water.

"It was uneventful," I said.

"The best kind," Elise said with a nod.

Elise had her own room here and as far as I knew she rarely left. She certainly always seemed to be here. I honestly didn't know how the household would run without her.

"How many days before you have to leave again?" she asked, pulling off her silver oven mitts.

"Three days," I said.

Bella came in through her cat door and sat down at my feet.

I picked her up and held her close.

"The young man who brought you home is back there with your Daddy," Elise said.

"Okay." Bella started squirming so I set her on her feet.

"Maybe he'll stay for dinner," Elise said, looking at me sideways.

"Maybe," I said.

I wasn't sure why Elise was telling me this. Was I wearing some kind of sign that told her I was crushing on Cooper?

I hadn't brought a boyfriend home since my high school boyfriend and I had broken up. And that had been too many years to even think about.

Maybe Elise was just being hopeful.

"What time is Momma coming home?" I asked, mostly to distract Elise from talking about Cooper.

Elise glanced at the phone lying on the kitchen counter.

"I think she's on her way home now," she said.

Good. Maybe Momma would be a good distraction to keep me from thinking too much about Cooper.

8

COOPER

*I*t was a little hard to concentrate on what Noah was saying. My gaze kept straying to the door behind him.

I knew that Wynter was here somewhere. I'd driven her here myself.

And I couldn't keep myself from wanting to see her again.

"You'll need to go to trainings several times a year," Noah said. "They're all over. Florida. Oklahoma."

"Right."

Noah had mentioned this in the interview. It was standard for pilots to continue their training and I knew that working for Noah involved a lot of continuing education. Working for Skye Travels was not one of those job where people came to coast.

"You're good with that?" he asked, keeping his gaze on mine.

"Yes, Sir," I said. "Of course."

"Good," Noah said, sitting back and opening a bottle of water.

I sat up, adjusted my cuffs, and leaned back again. Was I supposed to just sit here and hang out with him?

Going to the boss's home on the first day of work was quite unconventional.

Noah was more eccentric than I'd heard.

"You'll stay," he said. "Have dinner with us."

Was he asking? Or telling?

I ran a hand through my hair. I might as well play this out. See where it goes.

It wasn't like I had plans for tonight.

I'd actually planned on a late night, but not having dinner at the boss's house. I'd planned on being in the air.

"Okay," I said.

"Good. My wife should be home shortly."

As though on cue, his phone began to chime.

"I need to take this," he said, without looking at me. He pressed the phone to his ear and walked out of the office, his voice muffled beyond understanding.

I sat forward, my elbows on my knees. Rubbed my hands together. Maybe I was supposed to take a cue and slip out.

A couple of minutes later, Noah strode back into the office. Glanced at me, but walked to his desk and picked up his keys.

"I have to go," he said.

I stood up.

"I can drive you."

He stopped. Looked at me.

"I can drive myself," he said. "Besides, you're a pilot."

I nodded. I was glad that he remembered.

"Stay," he said. "Get acquainted."

Then he turned and strode out the back door.

A couple of minutes later, I heard a garage door opening and then saw his black pickup truck backing out.

I should definitely go.

I took three steps toward the office door and stopped.

"Where did Daddy go?" Wynter stood in the doorway, her brows creased, looking at me as though I'd done something.

She'd changed her clothes. Instead of the black suit, she was wearing blue jeans and long-sleeve t-shirt.

"He didn't tell me," I said.

"But…" She watched as his truck pulled out onto the street.

She looked good in jeans. More approachable. I imagined she would fit perfectly in my arms.

"He got a phone call from someone," I said, helpfully.

She shifted her gaze back to me.

"Why didn't you drive him?" she asked.

9

WYNTER

"He wanted to drive himself," Cooper said.

I paced to Daddy's desk. Ran a fingertip along the smooth wood.

"That makes no sense," I said to myself.

I turned, leaning against the desk, and looked at Cooper. I didn't try to hide my suspiciousness.

"Does he know you stayed?" I asked, trying to make sense of why Daddy had the driver here in the first place and, second of all, he left, but the driver stayed.

"He told me to stay," Cooper said, running a hand over his chin. "To get acquainted."

"Get acquainted with what?" I asked.

He lifted his hands, palms up.

"His words," he said.

I took a deep breath.

"Come on then," I said, pushing off the desk and leaving him to follow me. Or not.

It made no difference to me.

As I left the office and stepped into the foyer, I knew that he followed.

I went back to the kitchen. Elise was nowhere to be seen. But the pie was on a tray on the counter, with plates and forks.

I pulled a bottle of water from the refrigerator and handed it to Cooper.

After pulling a knife from a drawer, I sat down on one of the bar stools and slid the pie to me.

Daddy had been doing some odd things lately.

He'd been through a lot, so it was to be expected.

My three sisters and I had made a pact that we'd do what we could to keep the stress off our father.

He'd gotten through a bout of prostate cancer which was now in remission and we hoped to do our part in keeping it at bay.

For whatever reason, Daddy wanted Cooper here. Daddy had a propensity to pull his employees into the family fold. So I'd do what I could to make him feel welcome. It was expected of me. Drilled into me since I was a child. The youngest of four sisters, I had plenty of role models to live up to.

I carefully sliced the still warm apple pie, placed one slice onto a plate, and slid it toward Cooper.

"You might as well make yourself at home," I said.

Cooper was watching me with a perplexed expression. He didn't seem to know why he was here either.

Keeping his eyes on mine, he slid out a barstool and sat down across from me.

But instead of picking up a fork, he just looked at me.

"Aren't you going to eat?" he asked.

"I don't eat pie," I said with a quick shake of my head.

"Then I don't eat pie either," he said, pushing the plate back and leaning his elbows on the counter.

I closed my eyes for a moment.

I wasn't being a very good host.

With a sigh, I cut another—smaller—slice of pie and put it on a plate.

Then I picked up a fork, stabbed it into the pie, and looking at Cooper, took a bite.

He smiled a slow smile and pulled his own plate back to him.

I felt like he'd somehow won and I was caught in his lair.

Fanciful. That's what I was.

Cooper was a guest. And I was merely doing what was expected of me.

What I couldn't explain was why my heart was pounding so hard and I was having trouble keeping my thoughts going in a straight line.

10

COOPER

*T*here was something incredibly sexy about seeing Wynter eat a bite of pie, especially after stating that she didn't eat pie.

That small action told me a lot about her.

It told me that she wasn't selfish.

And it told me she might have rules, but she was willing to break them.

It also told me that I might, if I played my cards right, have a chance with this girl.

Her red lips were full and soft and... I shifted in my chair, I pulled my gaze away from her and focused on the flaky pie on the plate in front of me.

Even though she only ate the one bite, I finished off my slice. I had to admit it was damn good.

Not that I wanted a chance with Wynter Worthington.

I had enough girlfriends. Nothing serious. I wasn't looking for anything serious.

Wynter wasn't the kind of girl a man could do casual with. Even if she wasn't the boss's daughter.

I might as well walk into a wall.

"Tell me something Wynter Worthington," I said.

Her lips curved into a half smile.

"Tell you what Cooper?"

My name on her lips held promises she didn't even realize she was making.

"Does your daddy bring all his new hires home on the first day?"

She shrugged, sweeping her hair back and letting it fall over her left shoulder.

"When it suits him," she said, looking up at me from beneath lowered lashes.

I straightened on the stool. Leaned back. It occurred to me that this girl was flirting with me.

I was an expert in the flirting department.

And she was definitely flirting.

I looked over my shoulder, at what, I couldn't say. Maybe looked to see if Noah was walking through the door.

I hadn't calculated this into my plan.

"You shouldn't be doing that," I said.

She was going to get me in trouble.

"Doing what?" she asked innocently, with an exaggerated southern drawl.

"You know what," I said, with a shake of my head. Then I looked away. Looking into her eyes was like looking into trouble.

She stuck the tines of her fork into her pie crust and put a tiny flake of that crust into her mouth.

She was danger and I couldn't look away.

"I should probably go," I said.

She tapped the screen of her phone, bringing up a text I couldn't read from here.

"You can if you want to," she said. "But Daddy's going to be back in an hour."

"What does he want?" I asked, certain that she knew.

"I wouldn't know," she said.

"Well," I said, standing up. "He can give me a call. We can reschedule." I turned around. "Thanks for the pie," I said, over my shoulder.

Whatever Noah wanted couldn't possibly be worth getting into trouble with his daughter.

I went outside, got into the SUV, and pulled onto the street.

Maybe I could go home and we could start this day all over again tomorrow.

11

WYNTER

*C*urled up on the sofa with a novel in my hands, I watched the steady ticking of the large clock on the mantle.

The television was on, playing low in the background. The Weather Channel. It was somehow programmed to automatically come on to the Weather Channel.

Pilots were like little meteorologists. The weather was an integral part of the aviation world.

So I, too, had developed a propensity to always know what the weather was doing.

And right it was typical spring weather. Hot. Hotter than spring should be.

It was actually two hours before Daddy got home. He had Momma in tow. She looked a bit frazzled. Not enough that anyone else would notice, but she was definitely not in her normal cool frame of mind.

As they came through the back door, I sat up, putting my feet on the floor.

"What happened?" I asked.

"Car trouble," Momma said with a shrug.

Car trouble? That sounded a bit fishy. Momma could have called one of our drivers.

They were talking quietly, their head together, in the kitchen, so I stretched out again and went back to reading my book.

A few minutes later Daddy came into the room.

"Have you seen Cooper?" he asked, his hands on his hips.

He looked a bit baffled that he couldn't find Cooper.

I put the bookmark in my novel and closed it.

"He left," I said, with a little shrug.

The shrug was intentional. I didn't want Daddy to know that I secretly had wanted Cooper to stay.

That I had a bit of a crush on his new driver.

Daddy ran a hand through his hair. He looked genuinely perplexed.

"I asked him to stay," he said.

"I don't think he understood what you meant by *get acquainted*."

"He's going to be working closely with us, so I thought he needed to get to know us."

Maybe Daddy should have been more clear in his words.

"He will," I said. "in time."

"I'm thinking of assigning him to you," Daddy said.

"Oh. That's not necessary."

"He would be your own person."

What did that mean?

"I don't need my own person."

Even as I said the words, my heart skipped a beat.

The thought of Cooper being assigned to me for anything was admittedly intriguing.

I wouldn't admit it, but I wouldn't mind spending time with him.

"Well," Daddy said. "It wouldn't hurt. He could go with you. Wait for you."

"What?" Alarm bells were going off in my head. "What do you mean go with me?"

Daddy leaned against one of the oversized chairs. Picked up the newspaper folded neatly on the end table, but didn't look at it.

"He would go with you to your jobs. Wait for you."

Daddy was trying to give me a chaperone? I didn't mind living at home, but I had a different life during that three-fourths of my time that I spent in different cities all over the country.

The last thing I needed was someone hanging around reporting back to Daddy how I spent my time.

"We'll talk more about it," Daddy said. "Don't rule it out." He didn't wait for me to answer before he turned back to the kitchen, taking the newspaper with him.

I rested my chin on the edge of my book. I didn't have to think about it.

I'd already said no. Daddy, however, didn't take no for an answer when he got something in his mind.

If he was going to assign me a driver, I'd just have to deal with it.

All in all, sometimes it would be nice to have someone there with a car. But not Cooper.

Cooper would disrupt my concentration.

He disturbed me in ways only a handsome man could.

12

COOPER

The wheels touched down in a smooth landing at the Houston airport. It was late afternoon and the heat drifted off the tarmac in waves.

Two days in Denver, but I hadn't missed the heat not one bit.

I hadn't seen Noah for three days. Not since that day I'd driven his daughter home.

I'd barely seen anyone, actually. I'd had two long day flights and the one overnight flight.

I taxied toward the Skye Travels tarmac. Looking forward to a hot shower and a cold beer. Didn't much care which order. I had tomorrow off, so it didn't much matter.

I'd left my passenger in Denver, so it was just me in the plane. No car driving up to meet us.

I walked quickly through the heat, eager to get inside in the air conditioning.

I had some paperwork, so I had to go up to the office for a few minutes.

As I stepped onto the elevator, I remembered to turn my phone on.

I had one message. It was from Helen, the receptionist.

HELEN: *Noah needs to see you when you land. I won't be here, but you can go straight to his office.*

Great. I'd gotten comfortable. Thinking I was off Noah's radar.

Now I'd have to explain why I'd left the other evening when he'd expressly asked me to wait.

I would plead ignorance. Hope for forgiveness.

The elevator dinged and I stepped onto the third floor of the building. The red Skye Travels logo splashed across the wall. The same logo that graced every one of his planes. Designed by his daughter, Brianna. Or so I'd heard.

The office smelled like cinnamon and vanilla with a distinct undertone of jet fuel.

The lobby was spaciously furnished with two sofas and half a dozen chairs scattered about. Not typical lobby waiting chairs, but real chairs like a person would find in their own living room.

Even the two coffee tables had fresh flowers in the middle of them and that was it. No obligatory magazines lying around.

The receptionist desk was quiet, dark. The phones no doubt sent to the answering service.

It wasn't hard to find Noah's office.

It was the corner office with all the windows, his desk positioned so that he could see every movement outside on the tarmac.

He'd no doubt seen my landing just now. And I'd thought no one had noticed.

Noah sat in a chair, a newspaper spread out in front of him —an actual old-fashioned newspaper.

As I knocked on the door and stepped inside, he set the paper aside.

"Nice landing," he said. "Have a seat."

I sat in a chair across from him. This was the kind of chair a man could settle into and stay awhile.

Noah was smart that way. He made his guests feel comfortable. Let their guard down. Then he'd hit them with whatever piece of information he needed or whatever task he needed to have done.

If a man thought to spend idle time in Noah's office, he was delusional.

That was my take anyway.

Noah handed me one of the bottles of water sitting on the end table next to his chair.

I leaned forward, thanked him for the water, and sat back. The water was cool as it hit the back of my throat. I hadn't realized just how much I'd been craving something so simple as water.

"I have a request," Noah said.

No preamble. Fortunately, no questions about the evening I'd left his house after taking his daughter home.

I braced myself. What Noah called a request wouldn't actually be a request. It was a demand disguised as a request.

"Sure thing," I said.

Noah grinned.

"I hope it's not too much of an inconvenience," he said.

I had a feeling he really didn't care.

That he expected me to do whatever it was he was going to ask. Whether it was an inconvenience or not.

And I expected that I would do just that.

13

WYNTER

*J*ust as I had expected, my time off had flown past. I'd enjoyed the few days of having no responsibilities outside of family, but I was ready to go back to work.

That was one thing I loved about the way I spaced my jobs. I didn't get tired of working and I didn't get tired of having time off.

This time I was headed to Denver. Somewhere in there, I'd have to make time to see my older sister Madison and her husband Kade.

I'd just seen them Sunday, here in Houston for the family weekly Sunday dinner, but Madison wanted me to see her new house. She was seven months pregnant, so she'd been working on a nursery for the baby girl they were expecting. She kept saying that she wouldn't be able to fly much longer, but the pilot's blood she had running through her veins kept overruling that logical decision.

Not only had my sister been living in Denver for the last year or so, but my family had a cabin in the mountains, so I was quite familiar with the area.

I also knew that the weather in May in Colorado could be tricky.

So to say that I had not packed lightly was an understatement.

I stood just inside the door, waiting for the car to come and pick me up.

I pressed a hand on the wooden door and watched for my ride.

As the black car turned into the circle drive, my heart rate tripped into overdrive. I hadn't seen Cooper since we'd had pie together and he dashed out. Well... mostly he'd had pie. I'd had a bite.

Other than Daddy asking if I'd seen him, no one had even bothered to mention him again.

On occasion, Daddy would invite workers, typically new hires to the weekly dinner, especially during the spring and fall when he could grill outdoors, but not this time. Not Cooper.

It was just as well.

By the time I got back from Denver I would have forgotten all about him.

Denver had plenty of good-looking guys.

Picking up my leather computer bag and tossing it over my shoulder, I opened the door and stepped outside.

I watched carefully as the driver's door opened and the driver stepped out.

It was Jeff. One of the regulars.

My heart sank. I liked Jeff fine. He'd been with the family a long time. He was a family man. Reliable and friendly.

As much as I didn't want to admit it, I'd been hoping to see Cooper again.

"Good morning, Miss Wynter," he said cheerfully as he opened the door and waited while I settled into the back seat. "Luggage inside?" he asked.

"It's a lot," I said.

"Not a problem," Jeff said, closing my door, then grabbing my three large suitcases from just inside the door.

In my defense, I had to bring coats, sweaters, and boots. It was impossible to pack lightly for cold weather so I didn't even try.

The Worthington girls weren't known for packing lightly with the exception being Ainsley. Ainsley was a pilot herself, so she could somehow get away with only one bag. Probably learned how to do that in flight school.

As we settled into traffic, I reflected on my conversation with Daddy. He hadn't said anything else to me about assigning a personal attendant to me for my trips.

Thank God.

The more I thought about that, the worse I felt about it. It wasn't just having someone underfoot, it was having someone who would report directly back to Daddy on my activities.

As much as I tried not to be paranoid, I couldn't help but think that that was his ultimate intent. That or a bodyguard. But that seemed a bit over the top. I did just fine on my own.

I closed my eyes and let my mind wander as we turned off the freeway onto the airport road.

And damned if my treacherous thoughts didn't wind themselves right back to Cooper.

I would be alright once I had a change of scenery.

14

COOPER

*N*oah Worthington got what he wanted.

I'd known that when I went to work for Skye Travels, I might encounter some unconventional requests. I expected those requests to be for things like flying seeing eye dogs like Ainsley did. But apparently Ainsley had that market cornered.

Or maybe I would be expected to fly a bachelorette party somewhere.

But serving as a personal attendant to the man's daughter was something I never had anticipated.

Yet here I was.

It was mid-morning. Just before the first wave of heat torched the air. It didn't matter that it was just May. It mattered that it was Houston. Not even officially summer for most of the country.

The scent of jet fuel drifted on the heat waves, stronger with the heat.

Standing out on the tarmac, waiting for Wynter to arrive. I was to fly her to Denver. Stay in Denver with her.

That wasn't unusual. Pilots often stayed with their clients.

I'd even been called upon to be a woman's escort at a black-tie affair during a layover.

All sorts of things were to be expected.

But I'd never been assigned to work as one woman's pilot, driver, body guard.

In all fairness, Noah hadn't said anything about being Wynter's bodyguard, but I got the distinct feeling that she somehow needed one and I was expected to do it.

I didn't blame him. If I had a daughter and she traveled alone across the country, I'd want someone to be with her that I could trust.

There were so many problems with this.

First and foremost, I was a pilot, not a chauffeur, and certainly not a bodyguard.

And finally—I'm sure there were other problems—Wynter thought I was a chauffeur.

This could be quite a surprise for her.

Maybe Noah had told her about me, but I got the distinct impression that he was leaving that particular part up to me.

I had the plane ready to go. All I needed was my passenger.

When the black SUV turned into the gate and pulled up next to the plane, I stood perfectly still, my hands behind my back, hiding behind my dark sunshades.

I was not looking forward to this.

The driver, Jeff, stepped out of the driver's side. Jeff was the one I'd rescued that first day while he was sick. The one who'd been so loyal, he would have picked Wynter up, no matter how sick he was if I hadn't insisted on stepping in.

But he'd been grateful that I had. As a result of all that, my simply doing the right thing, Jeff had adopted me as his best friend.

He waved at me and went around to the trunk. He pulled out two suitcases. Then a third. Then a fourth.

How many trunks could one person need?

Maybe she wasn't alone. Maybe she'd brought someone with her.

I hadn't calculated that into the plane's weight ratio.

Jeff opened the back door and Wynter stepped out.

She wasn't wearing sunshades. I was beginning to think she had an aversion to blocking the sun out of her eyes.

She was watching Jeff and hadn't paid any attention to me yet.

I was just another pilot to her. So far.

I guess I was going to have some explaining to do.

After he closed the door behind her, she leaned toward him and whispered something that made him laugh.

Damn it. I was not a jealous man. But in this moment, I was jealous of the way she smiled at Jeff.

In the short time I'd known her, this was the first time I'd seen her smile. And her smile was like a ray of sunshine.

I'd like to be in her world. To experience that ray of sunshine turned on me.

But when she turned and saw me, her smile turned to confusion, then to a frown.

Just as I'd known it would.

15

WYNTER

*S*ummer wasn't my favorite time of year, but it came with the territory.

Houston was home and heat was just part of it.

I didn't mind the sun. In fact, I rarely wore shades. The sun might be bad for the eyes, but it was good for the soul.

As Jeff rolled my luggage toward the plane, I hitched my handbag over my shoulder and made my own way to the plane.

I missed a step as I caught sight of the pilot standing next to the plane, waiting for me.

At first I thought my eyes were playing tricks on me. Too much sunshine.

But it only took a split second to know it was not a trick of the light.

It was Cooper.

Why was he here?

Maybe he was meeting Jeff.

But… I glanced at Jeff. Jeff was wearing his chauffeur's uniform. Black suit and tie. Crisp white shirt. Cap.

I shifted my gaze back to Cooper. Black suit and tie. Crisp white shirt. Cap.

Gold stripes at the cuffs. Epaulets with four gold stripes. Cap with gold trim.

Standard Skye Travels pilot's uniform.

The Skye Travels logo was embroidered on his jacket.

Chauffeurs did not wear the logo. They were contract.

My thoughts snagged, even as my feet kept me walking forward.

I stopped in front of him. Tilted my head up slightly to look into his eyes. But, of course, he was wearing shades, so looking into his eyes was impossible.

I reached over and pulled his shades from his face.

He was looking at me with slight amusement now.

"What is this?" I asked.

He looked at Jeff and I followed his gaze.

With only two suitcases loaded into the plane, Jeff stopped and looked at us looking at him.

Then realization spread across his features.

"I get the confusion," he said. "You see… I had a desperately nasty virus last week. Cooper was kind enough to take my place and drive you home."

I looked over at Cooper.

"So you let me believe you were the new driver."

"I was your driver," he said. "And it was my first day on the job."

I put my hands on my hips. Then put his shades over my own eyes. Now he couldn't see my eyes.

"Well," I said. "We should get going then."

Jeff, gracefully bowing out of this conversation, loaded the other two suitcases onto the plane. When he slammed the door closed, it seemed to jar Cooper into motion.

He held the stair rail steady while I climbed aboard. Since I was meeting my sister, Madison, I wore white sneakers instead of my usual heels.

I went straight to one of the seats in the back and buckled

myself in. I didn't need help. I knew the drill.

Though I didn't need to wear Cooper's shades inside the plane, I kept them on. I'd kept them mostly to make a point. A point that if I didn't get to see his eyes, he didn't get to see mine.

Besides, the truth was, I was mad at him for letting me think he was a chauffeur. It threw me off that he wasn't who I thought he was. If I'd known he was a pilot, I—.

I pressed my fingertips against my forehead. I should have known. I saw it in the way he walked.

I should have paid attention to what my gut was telling me.

Making my point was backfiring on me.

Wearing the man's shades felt oddly intimate.

And I knew right then.

I'd broken my first rule.

Never crush on a pilot.

16

COOPER

I settled into the cockpit. Put my empty coffee cup in the trash bag. Put the headset over my ears.

Reaching into my bag, I pulled out an extra pair of sunshades.

I smiled to myself as I put them on and ran through the preflight checklist.

The radio chatter provided a familiar background, one that allowed me to go into my routine, leaving my mind to wander to more interesting things.

Like Wynter Worthington.

Wynter could wear my shades all she wanted. In fact, she could wear anything of mine she wanted to.

I would especially like to see her wearing my white shirt. And nothing else.

To distract myself from that titillating image, I checked in with Air Control.

Time to prepare for take-off.

Noah had no idea what he had done.

He expected me to not only fly his daughter across the country, but to accompany her wherever she wanted to go.

Did he have any idea what torture he was inflicting? What had I done to offend the man that he would set out to make my life hell?

It wasn't that I minded being around Wynter.

It was that I liked being around her too much.

I was supposed to protect her. Not seduce her.

But my... How I would like to seduce her.

I adjusted the shades over my eyes. Not my favorite pair. But since Wynter was wearing my favorites, I would have to deal with it.

She's the boss's daughter. Not a good idea to think about her like that...

I'd never had much of a problem shutting down unproductive thoughts.

I'd always figured there were enough available women out there that I had no need to date a girl who would create problems.

I kept my women at a safe distance.

Sure, I'd had a college girlfriend, Sarah, but we'd broken up and that had been my sign to keep my attachments casual.

Wynter reminded me of Sarah. Sassy. Headstrong. Sexy as hell.

And not the least bit impressed by anyone. Certainly not me.

Most women were attracted to a man in uniform. They didn't care what the man beneath the uniform was like, they liked him *because* he was wearing the uniform.

Maybe I was jaded. Either way, I was intrigued by the rare girl who needed more than just a uniform to get her attention.

Wynter was not the kind of girl who would do casual.

I checked the gauges, made a couple of adjustments. It looked like it was going to be a smooth flight all the way to Denver.

I settled back, looking forward to the flight itself. As far as what happened when we got to Denver, well... that was an unknown that I would deal with when we got there.

Wynter was from an extremely close-knit family.

I would do best to leave her alone.

But, damn, she was fine.

17

WYNTER

I had some work I'd planned on doing during the flight. Some reports to read.

Unfortunately, I read the same paragraph about six times before I gave up and just sat back, closing my eyes. The plane glided smoothly beneath me. Cooper was a good pilot. I could already tell. And I was never wrong about these things.

I couldn't stop thinking about Cooper. It was worse knowing he was just a few feet away, in the cockpit, even though I couldn't see him from where I was sitting.

It was just the two of us—together—in the sky. Away from everyone else.

I'd flown with a lot of pilots to a lot of places, but I'd never had such an awareness of being alone with someone.

It was such an odd, unexpected feeling. My father was a pilot. My sisters. Pilots were threaded all through my family. I'd flown with all of them.

Why would it be so different with Cooper? So intimate? We were strapped in. Four-point harnesses. We couldn't even really talk to each other, much less see each other.

But everything was fitting into place.

The way he walked. Daddy having him over at the house. The way he didn't seem to know what to do as a driver.

I'd found it endearing. If I'd known he didn't know what to do because it wasn't what he did... would I have seen him differently?

The white puffy clouds were like a blanket beneath us. I'd slid the shades up on top of my head when I was trying to read, but slid them back down to block some of the sun's brightness.

I hoped Cooper had others. Any pilot worth his salt had several pairs of shades in case something happened to one of them.

Something had definitely happened to this pair. Me.

I ran a hand over the folder I was still holding. I should probably try to read again. I had my first meeting with the start-up publishing company in the morning. If I didn't get this read now, I'd be up late reading it tonight after dinner with Madison.

I'd have to get to the room early so I could plow through these notes.

Thank God Daddy had let the whole thing about having someone with me all the time drop. A personal attendant.

That was the last thing I needed to worry about.

I attributed a lot of my success to my alone time. My work required a LOT of reading and research.

Even though Momma and Madison and I was all psychologists, we all did completely different things. Different skill sets.

Momma did counseling. Madison was a professor. And I was a problem solver.

I had to wrap a lot of what they both did into what I did. I had to listen. To understand what the real problems were. Then I had to do my research. And finally I had to present a solution to the company.

I absolutely loved what I did.

But it was a lot of hard work. I had to stay alert and on task. But sometimes, usually at the end of my job, I'd go out and blow off some steam.

Have a beer. Play some pool. Find someone to flirt with.

It was freeing to go out in places away from home. Places where no one knew me. where no one knew I was an heiress to a billion-dollar company.

No one cared. No one was watching.

When I went out, I was just a girl.

18

COOPER

*W*e had to go into a holding pattern for a few minutes before we could land in Denver.

There was some problem on one of the runways.

I hadn't flown into Denver very often, but it seemed like every time I did, there was some kind of delay.

I didn't mind the holding pattern. It gave me time appreciate the view of the magnificent snow-capped Rocky Mountains. Being from the deep south of Alabama, I was still stunned every time I saw the mountain range. Maybe one day I'd go into the mountains and explore. Maybe do some hiking.

It would be fun if Wynter liked that sort of thing. I ran a hand through my hair and gave a quick response to the control tower.

There I went. Wynter had slipped beneath my defenses before I knew what was happening and I couldn't stop thinking about her.

I'd spent most of the flight from Houston trying to figure out how I was going to navigate being her personal assistant.

Noah had said I was to fly her where she was going, drive

her wherever she went, and make sure she was safe while she was there.

I couldn't wrap my head around how I was supposed to make sure she was safe if I didn't have eyes on her. But I did know that if something happened to her while she was on my watch, there would be hell to pay.

He'd given me a credit card. Instructed me to get a room near her and whatever else I had to do.

I would put money on him not telling Wynter what he had in mind. Just a gut feeling.

The fact that I didn't have a reservation anywhere for the night was troubling in and of itself. Sounded like poor planning to me. And Noah didn't seemed that the kind of guy who left anything to chance.

What was I supposed to do if she told me to go to hell?

If her expression at seeing me earlier was any indication, that was exactly what she was going to do.

So I was going to be caught between doing what my boss asked me to do and what his daughter would allow.

I'd been in worse situations. I'd figure it out.

Finally getting clearance to land, I took the plane in for a smooth landing.

I liked knowing that Wynter was back there. That she couldn't help noticing the smooth landing. Being the daughter of a pilot, she would notice. She would notice and she would expect no less.

I taxied along the runway toward the private terminal.

Everything looked calm to me. Whatever had caused the delay must have been cleared out.

Fifteen minutes later I had the plane secure. I unbuckled and stood up. Stretched.

Then I tossed my shades back into my bag and moved to the back of the plane.

Wynter was already unbuckled and standing up. She had her handbag over her shoulder.

She was adorable in her jeans and short jacket. Just seeing her put a smile on my lips.

But Wynter was not smiling. And damn if I could see her eyes.

She was still wearing my sunshades.

19

WYNTER

The difference in the air was already noticeable and we were still on board the plane. It was dryer. But the scent of jet fuel was the same. The sense of urgency that came with being at the airport.

I wasn't in any particular hurry. Not really.

I was meeting Madison at a little bistro halfway between her office and her apartment. I was, in fact, going to be early.

The black sedan was waiting for me, but I didn't see a driver.

I turned my gaze back to the front of the plane and jumped, at least on the inside, when I saw Cooper standing there in front of me.

He seemed taller inside the plane and I was acutely aware of his presence, much like I'd been during the flight.

He was wearing that amused expression again.

And no sunshades.

I quickly squelched the wave of guilt that swept through me. We'd made it here just fine, hadn't we?

The landing had been as smooth as any.

I was already crushing on him, so that rule had been broken.

Besides, now that I'd crushed on him, that couldn't be undone.

So I would ride it out. Let it run its course.

It did put a wrench in my plan though. My plan to be over him by the time I was back in Houston.

It was hard to get over someone who was right in front of you.

It was only a slight delay though. He'd be on his way back to Houston and I'd have several days here in Denver. Plenty of time to get over him.

"Ready?" he asked.

I nodded once.

He opened the door and dropped the stairs to the ground.

The ground crew were already at work.

I hitched my computer bag over my shoulder and began to make my way to the door.

"Let me carry that," Cooper said.

I just shrugged and let him slide it off my shoulder. To be honest, it was a relief. The bag was heavy. I was used to it though and I managed, but, still, it was heavy.

I made it down the stairs and stopped, looking around for the driver.

Cooper was right behind me.

A member of the ground crew handed something to Cooper and, nodding toward the car, clapped him on the shoulder.

Then it seemed like everyone was moving at once. My luggage was transported to the car and Cooper held the back door open for me.

I stopped just short of him.

"Where's the driver?" I asked.

"Looks like I'm destined to drive you around." He held up the keys.

So it seems.

"Fine," I said, sliding into the back seat.

Standing out here arguing about it wasn't going to get us anywhere.

I pulled out my phone and dialed Daddy's number.

Surely he hadn't done what I thought he'd done.

The call went straight to voicemail.

I sighed and leaned my head back against the seat.

20

COOPER

"*W*here are we headed?" I asked, my fingers hovering over the GPS.

Considering that I knew far less about Denver than Wynter did, I would be relying completely on technology to get me wherever we were going.

She didn't answer at first. But after checking her phone, rattled off an address.

I keyed it into the GPS. Watched as it calculated my route and directed it to the windshield in front of me.

Wynter was still wearing my shades. It was unsettling for two reasons. One, I couldn't see her face and two… well…there was something sexy about her wearing something that belonged to me.

It was baffling how such a simple thing could create such a feeling of connection.

And it worried me that I liked it so much.

I tried to shrug it off. I really did. If she wanted my sunshades, she could have them. Maybe she needed them.

But I was lying to myself.

She might be the boss's daughter, but she was sexy as hell.

I swallowed hard and focused on the driving. I'd choose flying any day over navigating all these cars coming from every possible direction.

Turns out our destination was only twenty minutes from the airport.

"Is this it?" I asked as I pulled into a bistro parking lot, tucked behind an upscale shopping center.

When she didn't answer, I looked back. She'd slid my shades onto the top of her head and was glaring at her phone.

"Is this the right place?" I asked.

"Yeah," she said with a quick glance.

Fortunately it was early enough that it wasn't hard to find a parking place. I put the car in park and watched her in the rearview mirror.

She was obviously having a texting conversation with someone.

"Everything alright?" I asked.

She dropped her phone into her lap and looked at me.

"My sister is running late. You can just drop me off here and head back to the airport."

Right.

So now I had an answer to my question.

Noah had not told her that I was assigned to be essentially attached at her hip for the duration of the trip.

Him not telling her had left me in a bind.

"I'll wait here with you," I said, trying to avoid the issue as long as possible.

She slid my shades back down over her eyes.

I smiled to myself. She had this thing about hiding her expression down to an art.

"No need," she said. "I'm sure you're ready to get back to Houston."

I scrubbed a hand over my chin.

"Actually I'm staying here tonight," I said.

Before she could answer, her phone chimed again.

Good. I got a momentary reprieve.

Using it to my advantage, I stepped out of the car, stretched, and looked around.

At least she was meeting her sister here. Otherwise I would have had major concerns about Wynter being here. Alone.

21

WYNTER

*M*adison was an extremely punctual and reliable person.

But she had been working harder than ever, trying to establish herself as a noted professor at the university.

I read through the lines of her text messages.

She sounded exhausted.

It could have something to do with the fact that she was seven months pregnant.

Anyone with any sense would have taken time off. Not kept pushing.

But I would expect no less.

She was a Worthington, after all. And we Worthingtons pushed everything about as far as we could.

ME: *I'm here. Just let me know.*

The door opened and Cooper stood there, patiently leaning against the open door.

Patient was a relative term.

Maybe it was a bit strong a term. He was more like a cat. Still. But muscles coiled and ready to pounce.

And I was the prey.

Unfortunately, he had me mesmerized to the point that I could barely think straight.

On top of that Daddy wasn't answering my texts.

I'd told him I didn't need a personal attendant.

But he'd gone and done it anyway. He'd assigned Cooper to not only fly me to Denver, but to drive me, and then to stay with me while I was here.

He didn't have to answer for me to know that he'd gone and done it.

I looked at Cooper through my shades—his shades.

We were here and I was ready to do something besides just sit.

So I grabbed my handbag, draped it over my shoulders, and got out of the car.

The chilly breeze that swept through my hair was such a marked difference from the warm air of Houston.

One thing I liked about Denver. It had seasons.

Cooper closed the door behind me and together we walked to the door of the bistro.

The warmth of the sun was in sharp contrast to the cool air. That's how it was in Colorado.

Cooper opened the door and we stepped inside the bistro.

I'd been here before, though it had been a couple of years. I'd actually been here with Madison, though I couldn't remember the occasion.

As we followed the hostess toward a booth in the back, I slid the sunshades onto my head. The light was low in here and the dark shades made it more difficult to see.

We slid into the booth and sat across from each other.

I ordered a martini with extra olives and Cooper ordered a ginger ale.

"Thought you weren't flying tonight," I said as the server walked away.

"I'm not," he said. "But I'm driving."

I just nodded. Then to avoid talking about this further, I pulled my phone out of my bag and checked my messages.

Nothing from my sister and nothing from Daddy.

I understood my sister not writing. She was with a student. Though she didn't say, I had a feeling the student was in some kind of crisis.

But my father was a whole different story. I knew he wasn't flying today. So he was just avoiding me.

I decided I should write Momma just to make sure Daddy was okay, but just then the server brought our drinks.

I set my phone down to admire the pretty drink in the crystal glass.

Cooper held up his glass.

"To surprises," he said.

Though I wasn't fond of surprises, I clinked my glass against his. It would be impolite to do otherwise. Then took a sip of the drink.

It was perfect. Smooth. Not too strong.

I set the glass down and just as I slid an olive off the toothpick, my eyes met Cooper's.

I hadn't really noticed before just how blue his eyes were. And right now those blue eyes were trained on me. He was wearing that little amused smile again.

"You're odd," I said, leaning back in the booth.

Cooper laughed out loud.

"You really know how to pump up a guy's ego," he said.

I twirled the glass stem in my fingers.

"I don't think you have any problems with your ego."

He put an arm across the back of the booth and continued to watch me.

It was a rather heady sensation. Having a man's complete attention like this. Especially the man I was crushing on. That I wasn't supposed to be crushing on.

"You're probably right," he said.

I looked at him with surprise.

"I think we might be kindred spirits in that area," he added.

I narrowed my eyes at him.

"Where did you say you were from?" I asked.

"Alabama."

I shook my head.

"No. I don't think so."

He scoffed.

"I think I'd know where I'm from."

I just shrugged. Waited.

"Are you going to elaborate on that?" he asked, sipping his ginger ale.

"You say you're from the south, yet you are not a gentleman."

"Maybe not," he said, with a little smile. "But you're from the south, too."

I bristled. As much as I tried not to let him, Cooper got under my skin.

"What does that have to do with anything?"

"As a southern girl," he said. "Aren't you supposed to be a lady?"

Narrowing my eyes at him, I slid a second olive off the toothpick.

"Why are you here?" I asked.

Now it was his time to bristle.

I knew exactly why he was here. I just wanted to hear him say it.

"I'm doing my job."

"Not necessary," I said.

"We'll agree to disagree," he said.

I just looked blankly at him.

Daddy had hired him, so I wasn't completely ruling out him having a good reason for doing so.

Maybe Daddy had gotten into some kind of trouble and he

was afraid I was vulnerable. Not likely, but anything was possible.

"Do you carry a weapon?" I asked.

The server stopped at our booth to see if we needed anything else. We didn't.

"Why would I need to carry a weapon?"

"If you're going to be my bodyguard, it seems like you'd carry a weapon."

22

COOPER

"*I*'m not a bodyguard," I said. "I'm a pilot."

Wynter swirled the third and last of her olives in the martini she'd barely touched and looked at me from beneath her lashes.

"And yet…" She shrugged. "You're here…"

I kept my gaze on hers and she didn't look away.

Was it truly possible that she just flat didn't know that her father had hired me to watch after her? He hadn't even used those words. Not exactly. He'd framed it as making her life easier.

"Why?" she asked.

"You'll have to ask your father," I said.

She glanced at her phone on the seat beside her.

"He doesn't answer," she said. "Besides, you have to have *your* reasons."

I leaned back and crossed my arms. She was right, of course. I did have to have my reasons.

I'd turned down a job with a large commercial airline to take this job with Skye Travels. Granted, Skye Travels had the better reputation, overall, but Skye Travels was small. And, as I was learning, unconventional.

If I'd taken the job with the large airline, I would never have found myself in this position.

Things were done routinely and by the book.

Boring...

"Maybe I don't mind," I said.

I saw the surprise cross her features. I'd done some research. I'd learned that although Wynter was a psychologist like her mother and her sister, she was an industrial organizational psychologist. That didn't tell me a whole lot, but after some more research, it told me that she had different training. She wasn't a counselor. She was a problem solver for companies.

She took a slow slip of her martini. Closed her eyes for a moment.

"Okay," she said, looking at me again.

"Okay what?"

"Okay you can stay."

My brows creased, I studied her.

She appeared calm on the outside. But looking into her eyes told me that she had deep undercurrents. Undercurrents a man would be hard pressed to ever completely understand.

I hadn't expected her to acquiesce without more of a fight.

But I suspected that a lot of it was because it was her father who had sent me here.

Noah Worthington, from what I understood, had a strong influence over his family. He and his wife had managed to raise five children into successful adults.

And admirable feat to say the least.

When Wynter's phone chimed, she picked it up and glared at it a moment, then put it back down.

"She's not coming," she said.

"Your sister?"

"Yes." Wynter sat back and crossed her arms.

She was the youngest of four daughters. Usually the youngest would be spoiled. But I got the impression that Wynter Worthington was far too used to being disappointed.

"Why not?" I asked.

"I don't know," she said. "Work."

Determined to turn this around, I smiled.

"Good," I said. "What do you want to do?"

23

WYNTER

*C*ooper was a baffling man.

When I first met him, he'd seemed disagreeable. But now he seemed… kind.

Not the same man who had walked out of our house when he'd been asked to wait for Daddy.

But then, maybe I hadn't been so agreeable either.

I lifted my glass.

"I'm good right now," I said. "It's nice to just relax for a few minutes."

He looked at me with a strange expression, but then he just smiled.

"A woman after my own heart," he said.

I smiled to myself. So he said. But he didn't know my true motive.

"So tell me," I said. "How did my father talk you into being my bodyguard?"

"Not a bodyguard," he murmured to himself. "Have you met your father?" he asked, loud enough for me to hear.

"He can be rather convincing," I said, with a little grin. "I guess what I don't understand is the why."

Cooper lifted a brow in question.

"Your father also has a motive for what he does?"

"Oh my God," I said. "Does he ever. He does nothing without a reason."

Cooper ran a hand over his chin.

"Do you think he's in some kind of trouble?" he asked.

"What do you mean?" A spurt of fear shot through me, mostly because the same thought had occurred to me earlier. And his question validated my fear.

But Cooper shrugged it off.

"I think he just worries about you."

I put the last of my olives in my mouth. The olives were my favorite part of the drink."But why now?" I asked.

"I guess that's something you would know. Has anything happened lately? That you know about?"

"No," I said. I didn't tell him about Daddy being sick last year because it was something I didn't talk about to anyone. Talking about it made it real and, besides, he was recovered now, so there was no need to bring it up.

"I guess he might not tell you," Cooper said. "Might want to protect you."

"That wouldn't make any sense. If he was worried about something, it seems like he would especially want to tell me so I could be prepared."

Cooper grinned. "Maybe I'm your preparation."

I just shook my head. Seriously? He was going to flirt with me now?

I got a text message from Madison.

MADISON: *I'm on my way home. The guest room is ready.*

ME: *I made reservations at a hotel.*

MADISON: *Why would you do that?*

Why wouldn't I do that?

"Something wrong?" Cooper asked.

"My sister wants me to stay in her guest room."

"What's wrong with that?" he asked, leaning forward, his elbows on the table.

"Nothing, I guess."

MADISON: *I was hoping to have some sisterly time.*

"Where are you staying?" I asked Cooper.

"I'm supposed to get a room wherever you stay."

ME: *Can Cooper sleep on the couch?*

MADISON: *Sure.*

"We should eat before we go to my sister's. She doesn't cook."

"Okay by me," Cooper picked up a menu and opened it.

I wasn't sure what I had just done. But whatever it was, I blamed my family.

MADISON: *Who's Cooper?*

24

COOPER

*W*ynter was nothing like I expected her to be.

The girl was the heiress to a fortune, yet she didn't act like it. Not that I had a lot of experience with women whose fathers who billionaires.

We both ordered hamburgers—big juicy ones—with French fries. We even ordered colas.

No fancy white tablecloths with candles on the tables.

Instead, we drank sodas out of straws, used paper napkins, and listened to peppy eighties music blaring over the speakers.

As we finished eating, I leaned back. Looked into her stunning green eyes.

She sipped her drink through a straw and smiled at me with her plush, kissable lips.

Looking at me from beneath thick dark lashes, she had me thinking about pulling her close and pressing my lips against hers.

I shifted in my seat as the blood rushed to my privates.

Geez. I was like a teenager around this girl. She had me thinking about getting her out to the car and into the back seat.

"What do you plan to do while I'm working?" she asked.

"It depends on how long you're here." It was the first thing that came to my mind, though it wasn't what she was asking.

She looked at me sideways.

"At least four days," she said. "Maybe longer."

"I might drive up into the mountains," I said. It wasn't even something I'd thought about until the words came out of my mouth.

She looked a bit disappointed. Where was that coming from?

"That sounds nice," she said, running a finger along the top of her straw.

"But I'll be here if you need me," I said. I'm supposed to drive you wherever you want to go.

"I think you'd be bored out of your mind if you had to wait for me."

"I don't get bored easily," I said, with a little grin.

The thought of sitting and waiting for Wynter to get finished with work sounded as good a way to spend the day as any.

As a pilot, I was used to having long spans of time when I didn't have to do anything other than monitor the flight. And other than taking off, landing, and turbulence, that was mostly done automatically.

I liked the time to think that flying gave me. All the pilots I knew felt the same way. Why else would someone choose a profession that required spending most of their time alone? That would be like a psychologist who didn't like talking to people.

The server came and cleared our table. Neither of us made any move to leave. The bistro was getting crowded. In fact, a quick scan told me that there weren't any empty seats and people were lined up at the door to get in.

"What do you do anyway?" I asked.

She pushed her glass aside and leaned her elbows on the table.

"I look at any problems the employees and management might be having. Then I try to help them solve it."

Her eyes lit up when she started talking about it.

"Give me an example," I said.

She leaned back. Shook her head.

"I don't want to bore you."

"Did I just say I didn't bore easily?"

"Don't say I didn't warn you," she said.

I shrugged.

"Okay," she said. "Here's a simple example. Let's say a company is having a lot of turnover. The employees aren't staying long. I investigate reasons why they might not be satisfied in the workplace."

"I would think that there could be a lot of individual reasons," I said.

She raised a finger and winked at me.

"Very good," she said. "And often that's true. But something there could be something systemic that can be easily changed. They just can't see it because they're on the inside. Caught up in things."

"You really enjoy what you do," I said.

"Yeah," she said. "I do. I have a nice balance of interaction with people, but I don't have to get too involved in their personal problems. I'm not their counselor."

"Like your mother," I said.

"Exactly."

She sat up and looked around the room, then brought her gaze back to mine.

"Want to get out of here?" she asked.

25

WYNTER

*I*t was getting crowded in the bistro. The music seemed louder, the song itself buried beneath the deep steady beat. I didn't mind the crowd so much or the loud music because it put us in a little bubble all to ourselves. We had to lean forward and focus completely just to hear each other.

But it was getting late and I still had a report to read.

"Sure," Cooper said, looking around for our server and signaling him over.

His lack of hesitation told me that he was ready to go, too.

The server put the ticket down between us and we both reached for it. Our fingertips touched and it was like an electric current shot through me.

"I'll get it," he said, holding up a red credit card with the Skye Travels logo.

I pulled my hand back, letting him have the ticket.

"I guess we're both on expense accounts," I said, trying to keep my voice light. But I could still feel his hand on mine.

"Maybe," he said, swiping the card. "But a gentleman always pays."

I didn't say anything. I didn't disagree. Not if this was a date. Which it wasn't. I did disagree, however, on a business meal.

But we'd been sitting here for nearly three hours and we hadn't talked about business. Not really. Asking for an example of what I did didn't count as talking about business. It was definitely a gray area.

But since he had the red Skye Travels credit card, I didn't bother to argue. I'd used it myself enough when I was in college.

As soon as we stood up, there was someone there to wipe down the booth. The bistro was more crowded than it had looked from where we were sitting.

We had barely even gotten up before there was already someone else sliding into our booth.

As we began to weave our way through the crowd, Cooper took my hand. There was that rush again.

Spending the day with Cooper had done nothing to dull my crush on him.

If anything, it had made it worse. Getting to know him as a person left me wanting more.

All I had to do was to get to Madison's house where I was staying, read that report, and get some sleep.

Then tomorrow I would spend the day immersed in someone else's troubles.

I wouldn't have to worry about Cooper or think about him. I'd probably forget all about how handsome he was in his pilot's uniform. I'd forget about how blue his eyes were. And I wouldn't be thinking about this electricity that was running through me right now as he gripped my hand in his.

As we stepped outside into the quiet, the music became only a distant echo, the cool evening wind seeming to break the spell that had woven around us while we'd sat together in the bistro in our little bubble.

Still hand in hand, we walked across the parking lot to the car.

Instead of opening the back door for me, he led me to the passenger door and opened it.

When I looked at him questioningly, he just shrugged.

I slid into the passenger seat and he closed the door.

26

COOPER

"What's you sister's address?" I asked after I turned up the heat and the seat warmers. It wasn't freezing cold, but it wasn't warm either. It was cold enough that Wynter was huddled forward, rubbing her arms.

Even with the motor running, the inside of the car was deafeningly quiet after the loud noise of the bistro.

She gave me her sister's address and I keyed it into the GPS. I was getting the hang of these different GPS systems.

I was used to my BMW GPS and, of course, the airplanes had their own system.

With Wynter sitting up front, I wasn't feeling so much like her chauffeur. More like her friend. Or maybe even her date, though I knew that wasn't the case.

I'd heard her say something about me sleeping on her sister's sofa, but she hadn't said anything to me.

I was flexible enough that I could sleep on a sofa or I could find myself a room somewhere.

Flexibility was a side-effect of being a pilot.

As I pulled out of the parking lot heading toward the freeway, Wynter was typing on her phone.

Neither one of us had looked at our phones for over an hour.

"Everything okay?" I asked.

"I guess," she said, with a quick glance in my direction.

I liked it that she didn't lie and pretend that everything was great when it wasn't.

"Change of plans?" I asked, slowing a bit before getting on the freeway.

"No," she said. "Nothing like that."

I nodded and sped up as I entered the traffic on the freeway. According to the GPS, it was about twenty minutes to Madison's place.

"Your sister lives in a house or an apartment?" I asked. I didn't really care. But I didn't want the easy conversation we'd had in the bistro to fade.

"It's a condo," she said. "They moved there when they got pregnant."

"A baby?" I said. "That must be exciting."

"I guess," she said, staring down at her silent phone screen.

For whatever reason, Wynter didn't seem particularly excited about the prospect of her sister having a baby. She gave the same kind of response I probably would have.

Not the typical response for a girl, especially a sister.

But that was her business. And although I wanted to know what was going on in her head, it didn't seem like I knew her well enough to ask.

There could be a hundred reasons why Wynter didn't seem overjoyed.

Her phone lit up with another text.

"So my sister isn't home," she said.

"What about Kade?" I asked.

She shook her head. "He's on a flight."

"Alright," I said, changing lanes. "Do you have a key? Or do we need to go someplace else."

"I have a code," she said.

"She'll be home later?" I asked.

I could feel her looking at me.

She didn't answer as I followed the GPS instructions and made the next exit.

When we came to a stop at the light, I looked over at her.

She was biting her lip and tapping her phone.

"Wynter?"

"I'm not sure," she said, turning to look directly at me.

My blood raced to all the wrong places.

We were going to Madison's house. And no one was home.

I felt like a teenager again.

This was not good.

This was a dangerous situation.

27

WYNTER

$\mathcal{I}$ squeezed my cell phone in both hands, mostly to keep my hands steady.

I was nervous as a schoolgirl.

Madison had been vague about why she wasn't home. That wasn't uncharacteristic for her. Madison tended to be something of a free-spirit. She fit the mold of an absent-minded professor perfectly.

But last time I'd spoken to her, she'd been excited to show me the nursery.

First she hadn't shown up at the bistro. And now she wasn't even home.

I reminded myself that I was in Denver for work. Not a social visit.

I hadn't really given her decent warning that I was coming. Still. She'd insisted that I stay with her and not get a room.

It was good thing Cooper had GPS, because there was no way I would have found her condo without it.

"Is this it?" Cooper asked as he pulled into a parking spot.

"I think so." I honestly didn't know. It was a huge complex and all the buildings looked alike, especially at night.

"It must be close," he said with a nod at the GPS screen.

"We should go inside," I said.

"Right," Cooper said. "Look." He ran a hand through his hair. "I can go somewhere and get a room."

"Uh huh," I said.

Neither of us was making any move to get out of the car.

I didn't want to say goodnight to Cooper, but I had an odd feeling that if we went inside Madison's condo with no one there, everything would change.

There was no way I was going to get that report read tonight. I could get around it. I could claim that I wanted to talk to everyone first. Get their perspective before I read the report. Some psychologists did that on purpose.

I was wondering now if they did that as a strategy or because, like me, they ran out of time.

So that was my backup plan.

I'd be alright workwise.

As far as being alone with Cooper, that was another whole thing entirely.

I trusted him. That wasn't the issue at all.

He was fully vetted and everyone knew where we were.

Madison could be home at any minute.

What I didn't trust was myself.

Cooper's blue eyes crinkled at the corners. He didn't just smile. He had a Duchenne smile that lit up his whole face. I wasn't analyzing him. Honest.

It was just hard for me not to notice a genuine smile like his. Especially when he watched me when he didn't think I knew it.

It made my blood race through my veins and made me feel like I was the only girl on the planet.

I'd already gone and broken my first rule.

Never crush on a pilot.

I certainly didn't plan on breaking rule number two.

Never kiss a pilot.

28

COOPER

*I*t was dark now and the full moon hung low and bright over the distant mountaintops.

This view was certainly something I could get used to.

I could also get used to the way Wynter's hand felt in mine. Even now I fought the urge to reach over and take her hand.

I could also get used to the way her hair her hair smelled like jasmine. When we'd leaned close in the crowded restaurant, I'd just barely detected the soft scent.

The car was warm now with the heated seats. Neither one of us seemed to be in any hurry to get out in the cold.

At least that's what I told myself.

I was caught in a bind.

My job was to make sure Wynter got safely from one place to another.

I had done that. I'd gotten her to the bistro to meet her sister, but her sister hadn't shown up.

It had turned out to be more fun than any date I could remember having since... well... forever.

And now I'd gotten her to her sister's house. If I'd known Wynter was going to be staying at her sister's house and not at a hotel, I would have already made a reservation for a hotel myself.

But now Wynter had arranged for me to sleep on her sister's couch.

I wasn't sure what to make of that. Maybe it had been one of those spontaneous things that had been said before she thought it through. Especially now that no one was home.

I wouldn't hold her to it.

After sending a text message to someone, she tucked her phone into her handbag.

"Ready?" she asked, putting a hand on the door handle and looking straight ahead.

"Sure."

I should just walk her to the door, say goodnight to my new friend, and get back in the car.

That's what a gentleman would do.

I considered myself a gentleman. Most of the time.

This, especially since Wynter is my boss's daughter, was one of those times when I needed to tread especially carefully.

But there was something about her.

Something about the way her lips curved into a perfect smile and she looked at me with deep green eyes that seemed to see everything about me...

I didn't want to let her out of my sight.

I stepped out of the car and dashed around to open her door for her.

She put her hand in mine and stepped out of the car.

I probably should have let go of her hand.

Probably would have under ordinary circumstances.

But somehow she'd woven a spell around me and I just couldn't get enough of her.

Walking beneath the soft old-fashioned wrought iron street lamps, we wound our way to Madison's door.

"I think this is it," she said, checking her phone. "She sent me a code."

Scrolling back through her texts, she found the code and keyed it in.

The door immediately unlocked and she turned the knob.

I should just go," I said. "Get a room somewhere."

One hand still on the doorknob, she frowned at me.

"Why would you do that?" she asked.

"I don't know," I shrugged. "I don't want to impose."

"Okay," she said and my heart sank. I'd hoped she'd at least pretend to protest at least a little bit.

However reluctantly, I released her hand.

It was the right thing to do.

No one was home and I should just go...

"At least come in for a few minutes," she said, opening the door and stepping into the warm condo without waiting for me to reply.

"Okay," I said.

And followed her inside.

29

WYNTER

*M*adison's condo was perfectly clean and carried the clean scent of peony. Probably had a humidifier running.

It was a two-story condo with an open floorplan.

I flipped on the lights and the hardwood floor glistened in the soft light.

Madison's white Persian cat, Kit Kat watched us from the corner of the kitchen island. She must have recognized me because she came up to me and rubbed against my legs.

I picked her up, turned her upside down, and cradled her close.

"Kit Kat," I said. "This is Cooper."

She blinked at Cooper with lazy bedroom eyes.

Cooper reached over and scratched her on the ears. Kit Kat started purring.

Interesting. He seemed to have that effect on all the women.

If he scratched me behind the ears, I was pretty sure I'd purr, too.

"Nice place," Cooper said.

"Yeah," I said, setting Kit Kat on the floor. She scampered off to the food bowl.

"Madison has everything a girl could want."

"Is that so?" Cooper was looking at me again. Watching me when he didn't think I knew it.

I didn't elaborate. Instead, I walked over to her sofa and sat down.

"Not so bad," I said, thinking it would do nicely for sleeping.

Cooper sat down, too.

Kit Kat jumped into his lap, no doubt for more ear rubbing.

It couldn't possibly be good to be jealous of a cat.

But Cooper had his hand in Kit Kat's fur. Just like I wanted his hands on me.

I shook myself. My thoughts had gotten waay off track.

"I'll get us some water," I said, standing up and heading toward the little refrigerator where I knew Madison kept her bottles of water.

The last time I was here, she had several bottles of wine in this refrigerator, but with her being pregnant, there was only water now. Water and a couple of bottles of orange juice.

I pulled out two bottles of water and set them on the cabinet.

I needed to get a handle on myself.

Bottom line. Cooper was one of Daddy's employees.

My feelings had no purpose here.

I needed to quash this crush before it got out of hand. But truly… I leaned against the kitchen sink and looked out the window at the darkness beyond. How did a person even begin to go about extinguishing a crush? It wasn't like I'd started it on purpose.

That was the thing about a crush. It was young, innocent and fun.

Fun.

I closed my eyes. I didn't get crushes every day. I had attractions, sure, but that was different from a crush.

A crush was like high school. Full of hope and promise and possibilities.

It was like Friday night football on a cold Autumn evening with the band playing and the hot chocolate flowing.

And that was exactly how I felt around Cooper. Like a schoolgirl.

Maybe... Just maybe... I could allow myself to just enjoy having a crush on him.

After all, crushes were only temporary anyway. Right?

I grabbed up the bottles of water and went back into the living room.

Cooper was there, pacing back and forth, his phone pressed against his ear.

He didn't even see me come back into the room.

I only caught a word or two here and there, but his gaze was down and his expression was fraught with concern.

I went to the sofa, kicked off my shoes, and tucked my feet under me.

Trying not to overhear his conversation, I pulled out my phone and started reviewing some of the information I was going to need tomorrow.

He clicked off his phone as he turned and looked at me.

"I have to go," he said.

30

COOPER

*W*ynter's hair had come loose from the clip she wore at the back of her head, leaving a strand of hair falling across her cheek.

Her green eyes were wide as she looked at me questioningly.

She didn't ask me anything. She wouldn't do that. But her expression held all the questions I knew she wanted to ask.

Madison's apartment smelled clean and inviting. It wasn't very big, but it was spaciously furnished. Not cluttered. I liked it.

I'd been looking forward to spending some time with Wynter here.

But family came first. And in this particular case, it just so happened to be my family, not the Worthington family.

I was what some would call the black sheep of the family. My family owns the Abrams Bank and Trust with branches all through Alabama.

With four brothers and two sisters, I was quite familiar with the dynamics of a large family. I was, however, the only family member who didn't hold some important full-time position in the family banking business.

I hadn't completely escaped the family ties and wasn't sure I wanted to if I could.

What I was sure of was that I did not want to be tied down to a desk.

Never had. Never would.

However, when my father summoned, I knew it was important.

I'd explained that I was working. He respected that, but I knew that as far as he was concerned, Abrams family matters came before anything else. Another reason why I'd never wanted to be an integral part of the family business. It was far too confining for my blood.

Hence, I was the black sheep. At least until one of them needed me to fly them somewhere. Then suddenly I was no longer the black sheep, but I was the white knight coming to the rescue. This happened to be one of those times.

"You have to go now?" Wynter asked.

I took a deep breath.

There were alternatives. I'd summarily presented them to my father, but he insisted that he wanted me there to take care of it.

"Yes," I said. Actually first thing in the morning, but I didn't want to prolong leaving Wynter.

I had far too many things to do just in preparation. And one of them was calling Noah. I needed to know if I could use his plane to get to Alabama or if I had to fly commercial.

"Back to Alabama?" she asked.

"Yes," I shrugged. Wynter was a psychologist and I would do well to remember that. Very little would get past her.

Not that I was trying to get anything past her, I just didn't want her knowing who my family was.

That was the beauty of living and working in Houston. No

one there had ever heard of the Abrams Bank and Trust. We were far too small to be known outside of the small towns where we had branches. Three to be exact.

But if my older brother had anything to do with it, we would soon be expanding.

"It's too late to fly," she said.

I shook my head.

"I'm night certified."

She lifted her phone and glanced at it. "It's too late to call my father."

She was right, of course. I couldn't very well wake up Noah Worthington just to ask permission to use his plane to fly to Alabama.

That narrowed my options. I would have to fly commercial. Then take the family jet.

I turned and walked away from her, toward the front window as I checked for flights leaving tonight.

And, as I'd expected, there were none that I could make.

I would just have to get forgiveness.

Watching Wynter out of the corner of my eyes, I dialed Noah's phone.

31

WYNTER

*T*he clock on Madison's mantle chimed nine times.

For me it was a work night and normally I'd be settled into bed, surrounded by reading materials by now. I'd read until I fell asleep, then wake up, jump in the shower, and head to wherever my job was.

But tonight was different in so many ways.

First of all, I wasn't in a hotel room. I was in my sister's condo.

And second, I wasn't alone.

I was with the guy I was crushing on.

Then there was the third thing. The guy was about to leave me here alone.

All that agony I'd put myself through about him no longer mattered. He was leaving so he wouldn't be here to annoy me over the next few days.

And right now he was on the phone with my father. It was ten o'clock Daddy's time. He and Momma would be in bed by now.

My siblings and I never called them this late unless it was an emergency.

He answered though. I could hear Cooper talking to him.

It was interesting that Cooper paced when he talked on the phone. I didn't know if he always did that or if whatever he was dealing with had him uncharacteristically anxious.

And I wasn't going to get the opportunity to find out.

He stopped, suddenly, and looked at me.

"Two days at most," he said.

I couldn't hear what my father was saying to him.

"Yes, sir. It's very important."

He started pacing again.

Ran a hand through his hair.

"I agree," he said. "I understand completely."

He clicked off the phone and slid it into his pocket.

Then he turned and went out the front door.

I sat there. Frozen.

He'd just walked out. Just like that?

I thought we had a connection. And I'd never been wrong about that sort of thing. A girl could tell by the way a guy looked at her.

Well. If he was that kind of guy, it was better that he had gone on and left. I didn't need to have anything to do with him.

I should get up and lock the door.

Pulling myself together, I sat up, slid my shoes on, and stood up.

This heartbreak was the downside of having a crush. And I'd just decided it was okay to have fun with Cooper and my crush on him.

It was like I couldn't quite get my footing with him.

I was halfway across the room when the door opened and Cooper came inside dragging one of my suitcases.

Then he brought in two more and closed the door behind him. I had forgotten about my luggage.

He stood there, looking at me, one hand on his chin.

My breath hitched with the intensity of his gaze.

I hadn't been wrong. He was doing it again. He was looking at me like he wanted to eat me up. Only this time he let me see him.

My heart was beating much too quickly and I was finding it difficult to take a full deep breath.

My feet were frozen to the floor. I couldn't look away, much less turn away, and I couldn't walk forward.

The seconds ticked past, marked by the mantle clock. I lost track of them. They swirled into meaninglessness as we seemed to look into each other's souls.

Before I knew what he was doing, he strode forward, covering the distance in two long steps.

He gently cupped my chin in one hand, his eyes never leaving mine.

He was taller than he looked. A full head taller than I was.

As he lowered his face toward mine, my eyes drifted closed.

I could feel his breath against my parted lips.

Kissing was not new to me. I kissed whoever I liked whenever the mood struck me.

But this mingling of breath was different. I didn't know if I could take much more of this sweet torture.

When his lips touched mine, they were gentle. We just stood there in a whirlwind of seconds, our only contact was his hand on my chin and his lips pressed against mine.

The sensation was so very different from what I expected.

I'd expected heat, but I'd gotten embers.

He deepened the kiss. Lips only. No tongue. That took a level of skill most men lacked.

My body responded with longing that shook me to my core.

Then his lips left mine and he brushed his thumb across my swollen lips.

I looked at him through my lashes. I didn't want him to stop.

"I have to go," he said.

I nodded. That affirmation was the only response my brain could manage.

Then he turned and went through the door again.

This time I knew he wasn't coming back.

I went to the door and after flipping the lock, I leaned my cheek against the cool wood.

I'd just broken Rule Number Two.

Never kiss a pilot.

32

COOPER

*T*he next morning as I flew near Denver airspace, I swear I could feel Wynter looking up at me.

She wouldn't be, of course. She had no idea where I'd gone or where I was.

At the moment, I was flying through white puffy clouds that did nothing to temper the turbulence of this area. This had been one of the most turbulent flights I'd had in quite some time and we still had a long way to go before we landed.

The roar of the plane did nothing to quiet my thoughts.

My father and older brother were in the plane behind me, their heads, no doubt, bent together in some business scheme.

My brother had an amazingly creative mind when it came to business and he had not even an ounce of fear.

Not that he needed any fear. With the family's wealth and reputation behind him, fear would have been out of place.

The scent of their strong coffee drifted from the cabin. Both of them ran on caffeine like a plane ran on jet fuel.

My grandfather—my father's father—had summoned all of us to his home in Alaska.

Grandfather liked to say that he'd done his time and now he was enjoying the spoils of all that hard work.

Personally, I knew that it was nonsense.

The man would never stop working.

I didn't know what he needed us for, but apparently whatever it was, it required us to be there immediately.

My father could have hired any pilot to fly him to Alaska, but he insisted that since my presence was also requested that I should be the one to fly them.

I would have made sense if I hadn't been at work at the time. In Colorado. Across the country from my family in Alabama.

It also would have made more sense if I hadn't just found THE perfect woman.

I'd decided that it didn't matter that I worked for her father and her by extension.

I had broken my own rule about not dating where I worked. And I'd debunked my own theory that I could control who I fell in love with.

Turns out that was nonsense.

The head had nothing to do with it. It was all about the heart.

For once my heart agreed with my cock.

But family always came first.

And my grandfather wasn't prone to theatrics.

Of course, I hadn't seen him in over a year and it was always possible that his shit was starting to slip. I'd know after this trip and next time I'd be in a better place to decide whether or not I should drop everything to do his bidding.

Fortunately, my grandfather was one of my favorite people on the planet.

And he was probably the only person who could have pulled me away from Wynter last night.

The feel of her soft lips was burned into my brain.

And I knew that as soon as this family business was completed, I'd be back to her.

Noah wanted me to watch after his daughter.

He had no idea.

33

WYNTER

hat kiss.

OMG.

I sat alone in the newly furnished conference room of a small start-up company. Everything was new. The smooth wooden table. The plush leather chairs. The fresh white paint on the wall.

It was quiet here in the conference room, but people walked past the glass wall. They avoided looking at me, but I was certain I was the topic of the underlying buzz of conversation. Overdressed, I stood out among the workers wearing jeans and white t-shirts. The managers wore black t-shirts.

The company was growing too fast. That explained a lot of their personnel problems.

I could fix that.

But what I couldn't fix was the way my thoughts kept straying to that kiss.

Cooper Abrams had left an indelible mark on me.

I turned back a page in the printed report folder and started reading again.

One paragraph in and my eyes blurred again.

I shifted in the chair. I was replaying that kiss again. I'd been kissed harder and longer. Definitely more passionately.

But never with such controlled longing. He was like a lion and I was a helpless elk. Yet I wanted to be devoured.

I didn't know why he had left, where he had gone, or when he was coming back.

I'd fallen asleep surprisingly easily after Cooper had left and I'd had pleasant dreams, too. Dreams that I didn't dare think about right now.

But now he wasn't even here and he was distracting me.

I pulled my phone out to text Daddy. I needed to know what he knew.

But my next meeting was in five minutes. There was no time for personal matters right now.

I took a deep breath and stretched my arms at my sides.

Now was the time to concentrate on business.

Thinking about Cooper had to wait.

I opened my water bottle and drank deeply.

After today, I'd go out, have a drink, and forget all about Cooper.

That was never going to happen.

Not with a kiss like that in my head.

In fact, the last thing I wanted right now was to kiss someone else.

No one else could possibly live up to Cooper's kiss and I didn't want to ruin it.

I wanted to just remember it so I could play it over and over.

I should have listened to my sister Ainsley. She was the one who'd taught me these rules.

Never crush on a pilot.

Never kiss a pilot.

Rules were there for a reason.

My parents had made sure I knew that.

And when we broke the rules, we did so at our own risk.

It took Herculean strength, but I tucked all thoughts of Cooper into the back of my mind and by the time the first black shirt walked into what was currently my office, I was ready.

I'd be back to Houston soon.

Then we'd see.

I wasn't finished with Cooper Abrams just yet.

34

COOPER

*a*s the wheels of my plane touched down on the Denver runway three days later, my heart was pounding. But not from the flight.

It was from anticipation and not a little bit of nervousness.

I told myself I was just here for work. Noah Worthington was paying me to pick up his daughter and drive her around. Not so different from any other job. Except, of course, that I also had to drive her wherever she wanted to go.

Unconventional. But not unheard of, really.

Pilots were often asked to provide companionship to their clients on trips.

Providing ground transportation wasn't so much of an ask.

But there was so much more to just providing various types of transportation for Wynter Worthington.

I'd honest to God thought that if I kissed those inviting lips of hers, it would help me get her out of my head.

That had so not worked.

It had backfired. The longer I was away from her, the more I thought about her.

The more I wanted of her.

She was one of those girls that a guy could get tangled up with and never get loose.

She was like a siren calling me onto the rocks. And I went willingly. Eagerly even.

I taxied over to the private terminal, secured the plane, then found my car.

It was always an adjustment to go from flying to driving.

Something only another pilot could understand. That urge to just take the car into the air and bypass all the traffic.

That would happen one day. I was certain of it. First it would only be the wealthy, adventurous people who had flying cars. Then it would start to trickle down to others until one day everyone would be flying cars.

But right now I enjoyed being one of the privileged few who could fly into the clouds.

As I pulled into traffic, I admonished myself for thinking too much.

Just because I'd kissed Wynter like I'd never kissed anyone else, didn't mean that I had a reciprocal effect on her.

I'd be lucky if she even spoke to me after being gone for three days without a word.

First, I hadn't been able to call because I was flying. Then I hadn't known what to say to her.

So I'd just left it alone and decided that talking to her face to face was the best option.

I followed the GPS to the office where she was supposed to be working. I parked the car outside the building. A new building with lots of glass and green space around it. Trees, grass, and flowers.

Someone had spent of lot of money making this place look good. Lush even.

Wynter didn't know that I was here. I hadn't even told Noah that was back, so this was going to be a surprise for her, no doubt.

I liked it that way, though I couldn't explain why.

I didn't need to understand it.

It was like a primal need. To seek out the woman I wanted. To sweep her away.

Like Richard Gere in An Officer and a Gentleman.

35

WYNTER

I stepped into the breakroom and took a bottle of cold water from the refrigerator.

After the first day, I'd adapted to the culture and switched to wearing blue jeans. I didn't have any t-shirts, so I wore a blue chambray shirt, tucked loosely at my waist. I wore white canvas—red-bottomed—shoes.

As I twisted the cap, Peter McDonald stepped into the room.

He'd been dogging me since our meeting two days ago.

"Break time?" he asked, heading to the coffee maker.

Deciding he didn't need an answer, I held up my water bottle and turned my back to him.

He watched me as he waited for his cup to fill.

As I looked outside at the verdant landscaping surrounding the building, I tried to figure out what it was exactly that I didn't like about him.

He was a good height. Not too tall. Not too short. Lean.

He was clean-shaven, had short hair, and was damn good looking.

All in all, I didn't see anything wrong with him physically.

He had a charming boy-next-door personality. He was actually the kind of guy I usually went for.

"You want to get some lunch?" he asked.

Without turning, I shook my head.

"Can't," I said. "I have to…" work… make a phone call… "I'm fasting."

"Fasting?"

I felt him look me up and down.

"It's working," he said. "How about a salad?"

I shook my head again. Then turned around and headed for the door.

Since he wasn't taking no for an answer, I had to just walk away. Sometimes that was the only thing that worked.

Fortunately, he didn't follow me.

I blew out a breath.

I went back into the conference room that I was beginning to think of as a glass fish bowl. Maybe I'd start requesting an office with walls when I went to these businesses.

This one, though, had more of an open floor plan.

Finding truly private space would be challenging.

I liked the little company. It was going to do well. Just needed a few tweaks.

Twisting in my chair, I looked out the window again.

A blue bird landing on a flowering bush of some kind and seemed to look right at me as he ruffled his blue feathers. I didn't know if he could actually see me through the glass or not, but I could see him perfectly.

His blue feathers reminded me of Cooper's eyes.

Damn.

I knew exactly why I wouldn't entertain so much as a lunch with Peter.

I couldn't stop thinking about Cooper. I wanted to kiss him again.

As long as he filled my thoughts, the thought of spending time with another man was almost repulsive.

It was interesting, really, as I considered it.

The blue bird flew off, leaving me staring at a bush.

No matter how advanced we humans thought we'd come, evolution had most of us hard-wired to attach to one person at the time.

And I was no exception.

This would not do.

I was not interested in settling down. I was enjoying my life of dating whoever and whenever I pleased.

No. This would not do at all.

I turned back around in my chair.

I had to do something to head this development off at the pass.

Pushing the chair back, I stood up.

I was going to get over my ridiculous and unexpected aversion to dating anyone other than Cooper.

Cooper wasn't even around and here I was pining after him like a lovesick puppy.

I was going to go find Peter. Have lunch with him.

It was the only way to fix this thing.

36

COOPER

"*I*'m here to see Wynter Worthington," I said to the young lady the front desk. Her nameplate indicated her name was Maryanne.

She smiled at me.

"You work with her?" she asked.

"Yes." It wasn't a complete lie. I was her pilot and her chauffeur and in some ways her guardian.

Even if I had abandoned her for three days.

I was back now. My personal business under control.

Wynter was now my only focus.

"I think she's at lunch," Maryanne said.

"Already?" I didn't try to hide my disappointment. I hadn't thought much past tracking her down and getting here. But if she was going to lunch, I wanted her to go with me.

Nothing wrong with wanting that.

"I'll see if she's available," Maryanne said, sending a text and smiling at me again.

Seriously? This company communicated by text messaging instead of phone calls?

When had that become the norm for businesses?

I lowered my—new—sunshades over my eyes and put my hands behind my back.

It was a stance that usually put distance between me and whoever I was talking to.

I didn't need Maryanne wasting her time and energy trying to flirt with me.

I wasn't interested in seeing anyone other than Wynter.

She's not answering," Maryanne said, obviously not the least bit disappointed.

"I'll just wait here," I said, not moving.

"Sure," Maryanne said. "You can take a seat in the lobby. I'll let you know if she answers. Who do I tell her is here?"

Maryanne was looking decidedly more and more uncomfortable.

Perhaps my usual stance was working after all.

"I'll just wait," I said, lowering my shades just enough so that she could see my eyes, not answering her question. Then I slid them back into place.

Maryanne lowered her gaze to her phone and began typing again.

I didn't care. I was hellbent and determined to see Wynter. I'd wait here all day if I had to.

It was what I was supposed to be doing anyway. I had a lot of making up to do.

I walked around the corner and looked out into the work area.

The employees, young and energetic looking, were all wearing jeans and t-shirts. They were all younger than I was.

And I didn't consider myself old at thirty.

But to these kids, I was probably ancient. Maryanne didn't seem to mind.

In fact, she was watching me from beneath her eyelashes, looking a bit petulant that I wasn't paying her any attention.

I scanned the area, but I didn't see Wynter.

"Can I get you anything?" Maryanne asked. "Water or coffee while you wait?"

Keeping my expression blank, I lowered my shades again and looked at her.

She just shrugged and went back to typing on her phone.

There was no computer on her desk. How did a receptionist function without a computer?

I probably should have let Wynter know I was coming today. That would have been the smart thing to do.

It was too late for that now, though. Besides, it wasn't part of my loosely formed plan.

Then I saw her.

I hadn't recognized her at first. She was wearing jeans and a blue chambray shirt. It was the shirt that set her apart from everyone else.

Other than that, she blended in with all the other young professionals.

She was walking right toward me… but she didn't see me.

37

WYNTER

By the time I got back to the breakroom to find Peter, he was already gone.

Someone had stopped me in the hallway to ask me a question.

It was just as well.

I was already second-guessing my impulse to take him up on his offer to go to lunch.

I was feeling a bit sick to my stomach, actually. A sure sign that I was doing something I didn't need to be doing.

I stepped out of the breakroom and headed back to the conference room. Then, on second thought, I decided to go ahead and find something for lunch.

It was early, but I needed to take a break. To get some air as they said.

As I walked past, people stopped talking and put their heads down. I smiled to myself. It was funny to see the Hawthorne Effect at play. A phenomenon first noticed almost one hundred years ago still worked.

If I stayed a week or so, they'd get used to me and go back to their regular behaviors.

But for now, while they thought I was watching them, they were working harder. At least when I was around.

Lost in my own thoughts, I didn't see the man who stepped in front of me.

I stopped merely inches from running right into him.

Maybe it was the scent of his cologne, but whatever it was, my blood raced through my veins and I took a step back.

Cooper stood right in front of me.

He was wearing his pilot's uniform, without his cap, and he was wearing sunshades.

I swallowed and tried to regain my composure.

"Are you going to lunch?" he asked.

I nodded. I hated sunshades. I hated the way they hid a person's eyes.

How was I supposed to be able to tell what he was thinking when his eyes were hidden?

He muttered something I couldn't understand and took my hand, leading me out the front door.

The receptionist, Maryanne, looked like she wanted to say something, but seemed to think better of it.

By the time we reached the parking lot, my brain was catching up.

I stopped and pulled my hand from his.

"Where are we going?" I asked.

"Lunch," he said.

I put both hands on my hips and looked at him crossly.

"Maybe I had plans," I said.

He crossed his arms and just looked at me from behind his shades. At least I think he was looking at me. He could have been looking anywhere as far as I could tell.

"Do you?" he asked.

"Well… no."

"Good," he said, turning and walking toward his car, leaving me standing there.

My phone chimed, indicating a text message, but I ignored it.

Cooper had dragged me out here and now he was just leaving me standing here.

I should turn around and go back inside.

He hadn't asked me to go to lunch with him. He'd just pretty much told me that we were going.

I didn't even know if he was still on Daddy's payroll. I hadn't asked Daddy. I didn't want him to know I cared.

Yes. I should definitely just go back inside. Just skip lunch altogether.

But he was standing there, holding the passenger door open for me.

He lowered his sunshades and looked at me.

Crap. Now I had no choice.

38

COOPER

I had to let Wynter decide on her own.

The sun warmed the top of my head while the breeze was cool.

Only in Colorado.

The scent of fir trees was strong. Like a live Christmas candle.

Again. Only in Colorado.

Wynter hated sunshades. One of the few things I knew about her for certain.

I was pretty sure she was about to turn and go back inside.

I lowered the glasses and let her see the intensity of my gaze.

She turned around, but didn't walk away. I admired the curve of her butt beneath the long blue chambray shirt that hugged her curves just right.

Then she whirled around and marched toward my car.

She cut her eyes at me as she sat down in the passenger seat. I just smiled as I closed the car door and walked around to the driver's side.

"Seems like you've got some splaining to do," she said as we buckled up.

"Yes, Lucy, I guess I do."

She looked at me in confusion, obviously missing my reference to *I Love Lucy.*

"Thought we could talk over lunch," I said, backing out of the parking space. Sitting here gave her more opportunity to change her mind.

"Alright," she said with a little shrug, seeming to settle back against the seat.

I didn't have to be a psychologist to see that she was anything but relaxed.

I pulled out onto the street. I didn't even know where we were headed. It wasn't like I knew this city, much less this area.

"What are you hungry for?" I asked, trying to sound casual.

But she wasn't giving me a break.

"Thought you had this all planned out," she said.

"Unfortunately," I said. "We're way past the point of any of my planning."

She shot a glance in my direction, then just made a face.

"Sometimes I wonder how the human race has advanced so far," she said.

"I know exactly how." I stopped at a stop light and slid my sunshades on top of my head. "We have women to do our planning."

She rolled her eyes, but pointed to the right.

"Turn right here," she said. "There's a decent Mexican restaurant there on the left."

And just like that being with her shifted into place. Being with her just felt natural. This was the way it was supposed to be.

I pulled into the crowded parking lot of the Mexican restaurant and turned off the motor. Loud music spilled outside the doors.

I hadn't taken Wynter for a girl who would go for a loud place like this.

Maybe it was just my preconception about what an heiress to a billionaire company would like.

"I'll get the door," I said, stepping out and going around to open the door for her.

We didn't talk as we walked to the door where we were greeted by a friendly hostess carrying an old-fashioned clipboard.

"Name?" the hostess asked.

"Cooper," I said.

As she made a note, I wondered how within just minutes I'd gone from one office where the main communication was by text message to a restaurant that used no technology at all.

"All right," she said with a smile. "I have you down. Mr. and Mrs. Cooper. It'll be about fifteen minutes."

We'd already stepped inside the restaurant before her words sank in.

And it was going to take even longer for me to figure out how I felt about them.

39

WYNTER

I'd just been to this Mexican restaurant last night. It was close to the office and had decent food. And the margaritas weren't bad either.

Mostly I'd just wanted to get out of the car.

Being that close to Cooper had been unsettling. Especially after he slid his sunshades up and looked at me with those sky-blue eyes. It was almost like he could see into my soul.

I wasn't sure just how I felt about that.

And now we were in a restaurant with the kind of loud music that forced people closer just to hear each other.

And on top of that, the hostess had just called us Mr. and Mrs. and...

Cooper hadn't corrected her.

In fact, he hadn't seemed to have any reaction at all.

Maybe he was used to people thinking he was married.

I certainly wasn't.

I followed him into the bar and we sat next to each other on barstools.

"What can I get you?" the bartender asked.

"Ginger ale and orange juice," I said.

"Make that two," Cooper said.

"Guess we're both on the clock," Cooper said as the bartender turned to make our drinks.

"I guess so," I said, running a finger along the edge of the brightly colored tiles on bar. "So... does this mean you've decided to come back to work?"

He winced. I had to give him credit for that. I should at least let him explain.

"Sorry about that," he said. "I had a family matter to take care of."

And now I felt even worse. "Is everything okay?"

The bartender set our drinks in front of us along with a basket of chips and some salsa.

"Enjoy," he said.

Cooper tasted his drink.

"My family has a business in Alabama."

"What kind of business?" I asked.

"Just a small closely held company," he said, breaking a chip in half and dipping it into the salsa.

"And?" I sipped my own drink.

"My grandfather wanted to discuss a new venture."

"So that was an emergency?" I asked. There had to be more to this story.

"I guess he's sort of like your father in that way."

"Oh," I said. "I understand that."

When Daddy had something business-related that he wanted to discuss, especially with my brother Quinn, he had no patience.

Patience, I'd observed, did not breed success. Not in the world of entrepreneurs.

Even in my own consulting business that I ran by myself, there was no room for hesitation.

"So you're part of your family's company?" I asked,

wondering what role he might play when he was busy being a pilot in another state.

"Something like that," he said. "Fortunately, I live far enough away that I'm not required to be all that involved," he said, taking a drink. "Usually."

"Cooper," the hostess called. "Your table is ready."

40

COOPER

As we followed the hostess through the crowded restaurant, I noticed that Wynter attracted attention. From both men and women.

Men looked at her because she was beautiful and women did the same. Wynter had a naturally kind demeanor that put people at ease.

Most people. Maybe not me so much.

But I was the one with her.

And because I was with her, after people looked at her, they looked at me.

I got a couple of nods of approval from men.

This was nothing new to me.

I'd dated a lot of girls.

What was new to me was how it made me feel.

I felt a mixture of pride and possessiveness. The possessiveness wasn't something I usually experienced.

But I wanted Wynter all to myself.

We sat at our table and I picked up my menu.

Wynter, leaving hers lying on the table, clasped her hands together and leaned forward on the table.

"Not hungry?" I asked, hoping she wasn't one of those women had no appetite.

She was looking at me with a curious expression.

"I know what I want," she said, then smiled.

I nodded. Was Wynter Worthington flirting with me?

"I know what I want, too," I said, testing the waters. "I just don't think it's on this menu."

She hid her reaction behind a water glass.

"I think they take special requests," she said.

I nodded and set the menu aside.

"Good to know," I said, backing off. The last thing I wanted was to frighten her away.

I wanted Wynter Worthington comfortable with me. Comfortable and safe.

When the server came to take our order, Wynter rattled off her order and she still hadn't touched her menu. I was a little impressed.

"Make that two," I said, closing the menu I hadn't looked at anyway.

As the server walked away, Wynter looked at me sideways.

"I'm beginning to worry about you," she said.

I sat back in my chair, settling into the conversation. I didn't care if we talked about absolutely nothing. I just enjoyed talking with her.

"Why would you be worried about me?"

She shrugged and changed the subject.

"Tell me more about your family business."

I winced. That was the one topic I really didn't want to talk to her about.

"It's not all that interesting," I said.

"Are you kidding? My father has his own company. My sister. My brother-in-law. And me. Why wouldn't I find that interesting?"

She was right. Of course.

And even more important, Wynter was the one girl I didn't have to worry about just wanting me for my money.

In fact… maybe I should tell her so she wouldn't think I was after her money.

She would have learned to be careful about that sort of thing.

"Abrams Bank and Trust is opening a branch office in Alaska," I said. "And I'm chairman of the board."

41

WYNTER

I sat back in my chair. Hard.

A server set a tray of sizzling hot steak fajitas on the table next to us. I didn't even eat steak, but they had my mouth watering.

I couldn't say what I was expecting Cooper's family business to be. Maybe an attorney's office or even a limo service.

But a bank and trust? And Cooper being the chairman of the board? Wouldn't have guessed that one in a million years.

"So are you leaving Skye Travels?" I asked.

"Wild horses couldn't run me off," he said.

I smiled. Cooper had some unusual sayings. I'd think it was an Alabama thing, but Momma was from Alabama and I'd never heard her say things like Cooper did.

"How exactly do you plan on being a body guard and a chairman of the board?" I asked.

"Oh," he said. "so now you admit that I'm a bodyguard."

"Do you know something I don't?" I asked.

Daddy hadn't said anything to me about me needing a bodyguard. I glanced around the crowded restaurant. It seemed to me like someone should tell me if I was in some kind of danger. If there was a danger, I needed to be aware so I could make an effort to be more aware.

"No," Cooper said quickly. "Your father didn't say anything about you being in danger. I think he just wants to make things more convenient for you. And to make sure you're safe traveling alone like you do."

"I've been traveling alone since I was in college," I said. Though to be perfectly honest, I'd only kicked my travel up in the last few months.

"If I had a daughter," Cooper said. "I wouldn't let her travel by herself."

"Is that so?" Cooper's statement had my thoughts scattering all sorts of different directions.

One, he would be an overprotective father. And two, he had me wondering if he wanted to have children.

The thought caught me off-guard. I'd never seriously considered having children. My sister was expecting. And her child would be the first baby I'd ever spent any time around.

I didn't know anything about children and having children had never been my dream.

Why was thinking about Cooper and children twisting me up so?

Maybe he had a girlfriend and was planning on having children with someone else. A man whose family owned a chain of banks would have women lined up. Especially since on top of that he was a pilot.

Either one by itself was enough to make him a good catch.

Good thing I wasn't fishing.

He was looking at me like he wanted to devour me right here and now.

"You shouldn't look at me like that," I said.

"Like what?" he asked, innocently.

I straightened in my chair. But he was still doing it.

"Like that," I said.

There was only one way to get a man like Cooper Abrams out of my system.

Problem was I wasn't sure even that would work with him.

The server brought our food and as we ate, we looked at each other.

I set my fork down and drained my water glass.

The only way to get Cooper out of my system was to sleep with him.

I just hoped it didn't cause me to break rule number three.

42

COOPER

*W*ynter Worthington was sexy as hell.

The memory of the way her lips felt on mine was burned into my brain.

She was like a drug I couldn't get enough of.

A dangerous drug.

One that was impossibly addictive.

And one that was definitely illegal.

Noah had hired me to protect his daughter, not to ravish her.

But she had me wondering how I could talk her into not going back to the office.

How to have a little mid-day delight.

Unfortunately, I couldn't share these thoughts with her.

I had no idea how she would react.

Probably would suggest I take my ass back to Alabama.

But the more time I spent with her, the more I wanted her.

I just had to be cool. To bide my time.

Wynter pulled out her phone. Sent a text message.

Then she put her phone back in her lap and looked at me with her emerald green eyes.

"Work?" I asked, washing down a bite of chicken burrito with a big swallow of water.

"Yeah," she said. "I was just letting them know I wouldn't be back in the office today."

I coughed, nearly choking on the water.

She was a mind reader now.

"Why would you do that?" I asked.

Pushing her plate aside, she pressed her fingers against the table.

"Was thinking you could drive me back to Madison's condo."

"I can do that." I pushed my own plate aside.

Seemed we were finished eating.

"You have some business there?" I asked.

"Something like that."

I nodded. "I see." But I didn't.

I had no idea what she was up to.

Her phone chimed with an incoming text. She ignored it.

"You going to check that?" I asked.

"Nah," she said. "I'm not addicted."

I laughed.

"If you can go without checking that message, you're the only person I know who can."

"I can," she said.

"I bet you can't," I said. And I meant it. I'd never known anyone who could resist checking their messages.

"How long?" she asked.

"One hour," I said. I was purposely making it easy on her. Only because I liked her. And because I worried about her missing something important.

"What's the bet?" she asked.

"A Yankee dime," I said.

She stared at me a moment, then laughed out loud.

"Deal," she said.

I took out my credit card and handed it to the server as he walked by.

"No peeking," I said.

She held out her phone in my direction, face down.

"You keep it," I said. "If I keep it, it's too easy."

She just shrugged and slid her phone back into her handbag.

"You might as well consider this bet lost," she said.

I just grinned.

It really didn't matter to me whether I won or lost because either way I would win.

43

WYNTER

I hadn't told Cooper the complete truth.

He took my hand as we walked toward the door of the restaurant. It wasn't nearly as crowded as it had been when we'd first gotten there, but the music was still loud.

I had expected the atmosphere to be different at lunch, but this was Denver, not Houston, and I wasn't so familiar with the culture here.

If anyone said that regions were more alike than they were different, I'd have to disagree with them.

My phone chimed again.

What I hadn't told Cooper was that I had different text message ring tones for work and family. The message that Cooper and I were betting on was from work.

And work could wait.

This bet would have been a lot more difficult if it had been a message from someone in my family. I would have already lost the bet.

Of course, if the bet was a kiss—or a Yankee dime as Cooper called it—I didn't see how either of us could lose.

It had been interesting that his thoughts seemed to have been going in a similar direction as mine.

Only I had been thinking about doing a lot more than just kissing.

Still… kissing was an excellent start.

"Enjoy the rest of your day." The hostess held the door open for us.

It was the same girl who'd made the assumption that Cooper and I were married.

I looked at him out of the corner of my eye. His expression remained blank, but he took his sunshades out of his collar and slipped them on.

He'd probably forgotten all it. That is if he'd even noticed. But for some reason, the reminder made me feel a bit flushed.

He opened the passenger door and I slid inside. Sitting in the back seat was no longer even a thought anymore.

In the driver's seat, he lowered his shades and looked at me?

"Is your sister even home?" he asked.

"She's supposed to be at work," I said with a little grin.

He nodded, shoved his glasses back in place, and turned on the motor.

I didn't miss the little grin that crossed his features.

This was going to be fun.

"I've got some Yankee dimes to collect," I said, staring straight ahead and patting my handbag where my phone was.

He grinned.

"I think I'm the one who's going to be collecting," he said. "You've still got fifty minutes to go."

I leaned back in my seat and smiled smugly.

"Don't you worry about me," I said.

Maybe I'd check my messages on purpose just so I could collect on this bet. There nothing more interesting I could think of right now than collecting a whole bunch of Yankee dimes from Cooper Abrams.

44

COOPER

*M*adison's two-story condo looked like something out of the home magazines. A vase of fresh white daisies and pink roses on a table in the foyer. A fireplace with a bundle of wood stacked neatly next to it. A cozy throw tossed over the sofa.

She'd brought her southern touch to Colorado.

Except for one room tucked off the living room.

It had a big desk, two computers, and a wall of books. If I had to guess, I'd put money on this room being a selling point for Madison.

I didn't know a lot about Wynter's oldest sister Madison and I hadn't even met her, but I did know that she was a college professor who had reunited with her boyfriend from several years ago and they were living their happily ever after.

But right now what I appreciated most was the fact that neither Madison or her husband Kade was home.

Wynter had dropped her handbag on the coffee table and was standing in front of me with a rather challenging expression.

"How much longer?" she asked.

I knew she was asking about the text message she wasn't checking.

I glanced at my Apple watch.

"About twenty minutes," I said. It was actually twenty-six minutes, but I was giving her a break.

Of course, if I thought about it, giving her a break wasn't exactly in my best interest.

She just grinned, sat down on the sofa, and put her feet on the ottoman.

I waited, not sure what she expected me to do. The clock on the mantle ticked away the minutes.

Then she patted the sofa next to her.

"Might as well sit down," she said.

I straightened my tie, then went to sit next to her. It was a big sofa, so since she was sitting on one end, I sat in the middle, leaving plenty of room between us.

Leaning back, I crossed an ankle over my other leg, trying to look nonchalant and at ease.

At ease was the very thing I was not.

When had the tables turned, I mused.

She got another text message.

I looked at her questioningly.

She just shrugged, picked up a magazine off the coffee table, and flipped it open.

The woman had nerves of steel. I hadn't been kidding when I said I'd never seen anyone who could resist the incessant text notification.

She stopped, studied something on the page.

"Might as well pass the time," she said. "How about a quiz?"

"What kind of quiz?" I asked, wary about anything coming out of a women's magazine.

"These are actually some good questions," she said. "Ready?"

"Not really," I said, running a hand through my hair.

She smiled.

"Here we go." She glanced over at me. "What do you most look forward to each day?"

"Easy," I said. "Flying."

"Okay. Next question."

"Wait a minute," I said, putting both feet on the floor. "You have to take it, too."

"I'm not sure I have just one thing." She dropped the magazine in her lap and looked at me."

"Well then," I said. "What's the first thing?"

She looked toward the ceiling, giving this far more thought than it required.

"My morning latte," she said.

I smiled. She and I were going to get along just fine.

Then she asked the next question.

45

WYNTER

"If you had a crystal ball that could tell you one thing about your life or your future, what would you want to know?"

I dropped the magazine in my lap and looked at Cooper, waiting for his answer. It seemed like a simple enough question to me, at least.

Most people would want to know who they're going to marry or how many children they were going to have.

"I don't want to know anything," he said.

"Nothing?" I sat back and studied him. The question seemed to be doing the opposite of what it was supposed to do. It was supposed to bring people closer together, but it was like a wall dropped down between us.

"I don't want to know anything about the future," he said.

"Okay," I said. "Me either. Do you want some water?"

"Sure," he said. His expression was blank, but his jaw was clenched.

I got up and pulled two bottles of water out of the refrigerator where Madison kept her drinks.

What had happened to Cooper to cause him to have such a strong reaction to a simple question?

I wanted to know, but it was none of my business.

What I needed to do was to turn this thing around. Change the subject onto something lighter.

I handed him a bottle of water and sitting back next to him, I put the magazine back where I'd found it.

"You don't ever check your phone," I said.

"If someone needs me, they'll call."

I nodded. "That's probably about to change," I said. "with you being chairman of the board and all."

"Probably."

I drank my water, not saying anything.

"When you spend a lot of time in the air," he said. "You get used to not being able to use your phone all the time."

"I guess so," I said. "You spend a lot of time by yourself."

"I don't mind," he said.

Probably an understatement, but I didn't say it. I'd known a lot of pilots and without fail, they almost seemed to need that alone time.

It became something of a positive addiction for them. Something they needed in order to feel at peace.

"How much longer?" I asked.

He glanced at his watch.

"You can check it now," he said. "It's close enough. You've proven that you have self-discipline of steel.

I shook my head.

"I don't need to check it. It's just work."

He looked at me that way again, his deep blue eyes sparkling.

"So I won," I said.

"Yes. You won."

I tucked a strand of hair behind my ear.

"I guess you're going to have to pay up," I said.

Then… just to play with him… I held out my hand, palm up.

He looked at me funny. Then laughed.

46

COOPER

I took Wynter's hand and kissed her fingertips, then lightly kissed her palm.

I wondered what, exactly, she thought a Yankee dime was.

It was a southern idiom, but surely a Texas girl with a mother who'd been born and raised in Alabama would know that it was a kiss.

She lightly bit her bottom lip, but didn't try to pull her hand away.

Linking my fingers with hers, I scooted a bit closer to her.

"I guess we should have been more specific," she said, her voice a bit husky.

"I guess so," I said, smiling. "Fortunately…"

She raised an eyebrow, waiting for me to finish my thought.

"Fortunately," I said. "I don't see how either of us can lose this particular bet."

"That's why you picked it, right?" She shifted so that she was facing me.

"Do you agree?" I asked.

"Maybe…"

Then she did something that threw me completely and utterly off balance.

She took my other hand, holding both of them now and climbed into my lap, straddling me.

Grinning at my shocked expression, she swayed forward, inches from my face, and closed her eyes.

Ah hell.

I'd known Wynter Worthington was trouble the minute I laid eyes on her.

But she was such a delicious trouble. Impossible for me to resist.

I closed the small distance remaining between us and placed my lips on hers.

We sat together, neither of us moving, as the sensation of that contact flowed through us.

Unable to do stand it any longer, I pulled my hands from hers and wrapped my arms around her, pulling her against me.

I deepened the kiss and she matched me, breath for breath.

My fingers tangled in her hair, soft as silk, and my palm splayed across her cheek.

My thumb replaced my lips, caressing her lips, for a second and my breath hitched.

Then my lips were on hers again.

My God. I couldn't get close enough to her.

I put both my hands on her butt and pulled her against my hard as steel cock. She'd have no doubt whatsoever the effect she had on me.

She groaned and ground her soft core against my hardness.

I shifted and laid her back on the sofa beneath me. I ran a hand beneath her long blue shirt and found a lacy bra beneath it.

Her hips tilted upwards and I ground my cock down against her in little circles.

Gasping, she pulled at my hair.

Then she whimpered and went limp.

I pulled back and looked at her relaxed, face, her eyes closed and a little smile on her swollen lips.

For all that was holy, I swore to myself.

I'd just made Wynter Worthington come.

47

WYNTER

I woke encircled in Cooper's arms, snuggled with my back against him.

The clock over my sister's mantle chimed three times.

The afternoon sun streamed through her living room window.

Cooper kissed me on the cheek.

"Hi," he said.

"Hi."

Sitting up, I stretched and the memory of that orgasm flowed back.

I looked over my shoulder at him. He was wearing what looked a lot to me like a smug expression.

I grabbed my handbag off the coffee table and pulled out my phone.

"Aha," he said.

I had half a dozen text messages, all work related. Two from this firm in Denver where I'd played hooky this afternoon, three from a previous job, and one a new job query. Nothing urgent.

"Aha what?" I asked, absently.

"Aha. As in the first thing you did when you woke up was to check your text messages."

Setting my phone aside, I turned back toward him.

"Yeah," I said. "And how long has it been since you looked at your phone?"

He picked up his phone from the back of the sofa.

"As a matter of fact, I was texting your father while you slept."

"Well, that's what a girl wants to hear from her boyfriend."

His eyes widened and I had to turn away to hide my smile at his surprised expression.

He grabbed me by the waist and pulled me back toward him.

"Well then," he said. "This boyfriend would like more kisses."

"No. No," I said, holding up a finger.

He froze.

"Only Yankee dimes for you," I said.

Then before I knew what he was doing, he'd swooped me up in his lap and, holding me close, had his lips on mine.

His lips were soft and possessive and oh so very tantalizing.

I was matching him kiss for kiss. He ran his tongue along my teeth, then he touched his tongue on the roof of my mouth and I melted.

I could kiss this man all day long, then all night long.

I was beginning to think I could live off his kisses alone.

His hands tangled in my hair, keeping me close.

I reached down, planning to touch him down there, but he put a hand over mine, stopping me.

Pulling back, I looked questioningly at him, my eyes barely open.

Smiling, he tucked a strand of my hair behind an ear with his other hand.

"Some things are better when there's a little anticipation," he said.

Seriously? How was it that I had found the one man who wanted to go slow?

Just when I'd decided that I wanted to sleep with him.

I moved my hand up to lightly stroke his earlobe.

"Is that allowed?" I murmured against his lips.

"You're trouble, Wynter Worthington," he said, claiming my lips with his again.

He had no idea just how much trouble.

There was nothing I liked better than a good challenge.

48

COOPER

An hour later, I sat on the sofa with Wynter sitting very properly beside me.

A very pregnant Madison Worthington sat across from us.

She'd barely blinked when Wynter had introduced me as her new boyfriend.

This was the second time she'd referred to me that way, but somehow it seemed significant to me to be introduced as someone's boyfriend.

Maybe it meant something different to Wynter. Or maybe she had so many boyfriends that Madison wasn't surprised to meet another one.

A girl like Wynter would have boyfriends. It wouldn't be natural if she didn't. Besides being beautiful physically, she had a smile that lit up the room.

Any man... any single, straight man... would be crazy not to be in love with her at first sight.

"Did you work today?" Madison asked, looking pointedly at Wynter.

"I did," Wynter said, keeping her gaze steady on her sister.

Madison just nodded, but I got the feeling she didn't really believe Wynter.

It would be hard to miss that Wynter looked like she'd spent the afternoon being kissed and kissed thoroughly.

Her hair was mussed and her lips were swollen, but she didn't try to hide it. On the contrary, she was wearing what looked to me like a rather satisfied little smile.

"Do you want to see the baby's room?" Madison asked.

"Sure." Wynter looked at me. "Do you want to come?"

"You go ahead," I said. "I need to call your father."

Wynter winced, but left me alone and followed her sister upstairs.

"Should you be climbing these stairs?" I heard her ask her sister.

"Exercise is good for me," Madison said before they were out of earshot.

The cat, Kit Kat, who'd made herself scarce all afternoon sat in the floor staring at me with big golden eyes.

"What?" I asked her.

She licked a paw in response.

"That's what I thought."

I walked outside, closing the door behind me.

The early evening air was chilly, but I found it energizing. I walked down the sidewalk, lined with old-fashioned lanterns that came on, one by one, as the sun set over the mountains.

Bright reds and golds splashed along the horizon outlining the jagged mountain tops.

Tomorrow was Saturday. It might be a good day to go up into the mountains. Maybe take a hike.

I stopped and sent Noah a quick text.

ME: *Call if you need to. But everything is good here. Wynter is with Madison.*

I felt like I was betraying Wynter's trust by reporting to her father, but I was only doing my job. And I hadn't told Noah anything other than harmless information.

She was with her sister. And she was fine.

He didn't need to know that we'd spent the afternoon making out on Madison's sofa.

Walking again, beneath one of those spruce trees that made Colorado smell like no other place, I wondered if Noah would fire me if he knew that Wynter was calling me her boyfriend.

Would Madison tell their father?

And if Noah did fire me, would that change anything?

Not in my mind, I decided as two chipmunks darted in front of me.

The only thing it would change was that I would no longer be paid for driving Wynter around and making sure she was safe.

The thing was… I would do it anyway.

Wynter had hooked me.

Whether that was her intent or not, I had no idea, but I was most definitely hooked.

49

WYNTER

"*B*oyfriend?" Madison asked once we were inside the nursery painted with blue walls, two light blue and two dark blue.

Madison had done the thing I didn't think I would. She knew the sex of her baby.

I suppose it was one of those practical things that made preparation easier. But, for me, I think I would be a bit old-fashioned about it and want to wait until the baby was born.

The fact that Madison had me even thinking about how I would be if I had children of my own was a bit disconcerting.

Mostly because I knew that it really had nothing to do with Madison.

It was Cooper.

Cooper had my thoughts all twisted up.

I'd had boyfriends since I was fourteen. That's when Jeff from next door had kissed me. We were both fourteen at the time.

It hadn't gone anywhere. Just one of those fleeting things.

Actually, I'd only had one boyfriend who wasn't fleeting. My high school boyfriend had lasted for two years and looking back we probably should have gotten married.

But I was the one who wasn't ready. I wanted to get out there and experience the world.

The world had given me many boyfriends, but none of them had lasted.

I shrugged.

"He's a boy. And a friend."

Madison narrowed her eyes at me.

Sometimes it was hard to talk to a sister who analyzed people for a living.

"You don't usually call boys who are friends boyfriends," she said.

"I know," I said, grinning.

"You like him," Madison said.

"Of course I like him," I said. "I wouldn't kiss him if I didn't."

Madison didn't say anything, but I could see that she was waiting for me to elaborate.

"What is this?" I asked, running a hand along a mat.

"It's an aquadoodle mat," Madison said.

"What's that for?" I asked.

"So he can draw and explore his creativity."

"You do know it's going to be awhile before you can start teaching him things, right?"

Madison smiled. "I know. It was a gift from my students."

"That makes sense," I said, sweeping a hand around the room. "Looks like you've thought of everything."

And she had. Everything from a cradle to a changing table to a stack of diapers.

"Want to know the truth?" Madison asked.

"Of course," I said.

Madison ran a hand over her stomach.

"I'm scared. I'm so afraid that I won't be able to handle being a mother."

"Madison," I said, going to my big sister and taking both her hands in mine. "You are going to be an absolutely wonderful mother. And you and Kade... You two are perfect."

"I know," Madison said, tearing up. "It's the hormones. I can't help it."

I hugged my sister.

And in that moment I envied her.

I envied that my sister had a fairy tale life that took the luster off my life of playing the field.

With three older sisters, I always thought I had all the time in the world to think about my future. But now that two of them were married and the other one was engaged, I suddenly felt like I was lagging behind.

Maybe I didn't have all the time in the world.

I didn't want to be one of those women who grew old alone. I wanted what my sisters had.

I had just never thought it was time to worry about it.

"Madison," I pulled out one of the little miniature chairs painted bright yellow and sat down. "How did you know that Kade was the man you wanted to marry?"

Madison sat down next to me. Sitting that low couldn't have been an easy feat, but she made it look easy.

"I always knew," she said. "From the first time I saw him."

She looked at me with a knowing little smile.

"Wynter," she said. "you know when it's real. Just listen to your heart, not your head."

She made it sound so easy. And I knew that for her, it had been. It had just taken her and Kade awhile to get it all together to make it work.

I didn't want that. I didn't want to find the right man, then have to wait miserably for years to figure it out.

That wasn't the way I operated. If something was right, I saw no need to wait. It was the way I was built. I lived by my own slogan *Tomorrow Never Comes.* I attributed it to how I'd been so successful in my business. That and my *can do* attitude.

I didn't hesitate when I thought something was right.

As long it fell within the parameters of my goals and rules, I just did what I needed to do be successful.

I'd never really gone about applying this to my relationships.

After high school, I'd decided that I didn't need to have just one boyfriend. I had lots of boyfriends. Some of them I had worked with over the years. Some of them not.

Some of them I still saw. Some of them I didn't.

But there was one thing common with all of them.

Not one of them had ever made me feel like Cooper did.

50

COOPER

I was heading back toward Madison's condo when Noah called. I stopped and stood next to a spruce tree that looked to me like a perfect Christmas tree.

"Hello," I said, wondering if everyone around here took the trees for granted or if they decorated them for Christmas. Back home, in the small town where I'd grown up, the people would go crazy with decorations for trees like this. They'd have the whole place lit up.

"I need you to come back to Houston," Noah said.

I held the phone away from my ear and looked at it.

Surely I'd misunderstood.

I put the phone back to my ear.

"I just got here this morning," I said.

"I know," Noah said. "But something's come up and I need you to take a flight to Alabama.

I bit my tongue. I'd literally flown back from Alabama this morning. And Noah knew that. I'd flown his plane.

I started pacing. It was what I did when I had something I had to figure out.

"I don't understand," I said.

I could almost hear Noah taking a deep breath and letting it out slowly. It wasn't possible for me to win in this situation.

"When do you need me?" I asked. Noah was the boss. As long as I wanted to work for him, I had to work the jobs he assigned me.

"In the morning," Noah said. "You'll need to go ahead and fly back so you can leave first thing tomorrow."

"Okay," I said. Damn. Damn. Damn. It still didn't make any sense to me.

"What about Wynter?" I asked.

Noah didn't answer at first. I almost thought he didn't hear me.

"She'll be okay," Noah said. "I have a driver on standby."

"Is something wrong, Sir?" I asked.

"They had to take Savannah's mother to the hospital. I'd fly her myself, but I had a procedure done on one of my eyes this morning. Bad timing. You're the best pilot I have available for tomorrow."

Damn. Noah had just wrapped a helluva compliment into all this.

"I'm sorry," I said. "I'll let Wynter know, then I'll submit a flight plan."

"The flight plan is already done," Noah said. "You leave in two hours."

Of course he already had that done. Noah was nothing if not thorough. It's how he'd built an empire out of nothing.

We disconnected and I walked back toward Madison's condo.

This evening had not gone as planned. Not even a little bit.

I'd been thinking about taking her for a nice dinner. A bottle of wine.

A woman like Wynter deserved more than just a tumble on the sofa.

That was why I'd stopped her from going any further. It wasn't that I didn't want to. I wanted to. More than anything.

But she deserved more. So much more.

Wynter was waiting for me when I stepped back inside.

Apparently Noah had already told her he was calling me back to Houston. Either that or she'd found out that her grandmother was in the hospital.

Or both.

Either way, she was looking at me like she thought I had something to do with this whole situation.

51

WYNTER

Three Days Later

Istared out the window as we approached the
Houston airport.

As the tops of the trees came into view, I blew out a breath.

We were almost home.

But coming home was feeling a whole different this time
than it had the last time I'd flown in.

Last time I'd had the unexpected surprise of a new driver
who wasn't actually a driver.

But right now Cooper was in Alabama getting ready to fly
Momma home.

Grandmamma had been released from the hospital
yesterday.

Everyone, including Grandmamma, thought she was having
a heart attack. Instead she had something called
costochondritis. Some kind of painful arthritis in the chest.

The doctors had sent her home with orders to get lots of

rest. I'm pretty sure Momma would have stayed with her longer, but Momma had patients. The longer she was away, the more difficult it was to reschedule and catch up.

Momma had hired around the clock caregivers to help with things around the house.

Grandmamma wasn't going to like not doing things for herself.

As the plane started its final descent, the freeway beneath us, I thought about flying out to visit my grandmother. It was the right thing to do.

I sighed. I had another job starting Friday, so I only had a couple of days to get ready for the next trip. A day spent flying to Alabama and back hadn't been in my plans.

As we taxied toward the runway, I saw Jeff waiting for me next to the car.

Jeff was a good man and I felt bad for being disappointed that he was the one driving me today. He was one of the best drivers.

He just wasn't Cooper.

The last three days had been trying in a number of ways. I'd been on pins and needles worrying about Grandmamma. And, although I understood why Daddy had wanted Cooper to be the one to fly Momma out to Alabama, I hadn't been able to get him off my mind.

His kiss had kept me awake at night. And distracted during the day.

My plan to get him out of my system by sleeping with him had gone sideways. First of all, he'd slowed me down. And I'd been too besotted with his kisses to complain.

So since I hadn't slept with him... Did having an orgasm count? If it did, my plan had most definitely backfired.

Maybe it was a good thing I hadn't actually slept with him.

The plane came to a stop in front of the Skye Travels building.

I sighed and leaned back against the seat as the pilot secured the plane for deplaning.

Cooper had said I was trouble. But from my perspective, he was the one causing trouble.

Because of him, I'd broken my first rule: Never crush on a pilot. My second rule: Never kiss a pilot.

Now I couldn't get him out of my mind. And I definitely wanted to kiss him again.

In fact, he was all I could think about.

A couple of minutes later, I unbuckled and went to the stairs leading to the tarmac.

I froze just as went to take the first step down.

Cooper was standing at the bottom of the stairs, grinning up at me.

52

COOPER

*T*he scent of jet fuel filled the heated afternoon Houston air. It was only May, but the light breezy wind already smelled like summer.

I'd watched the little plane starting as a little speck coming from the east. After it landed and taxied over to the runway, I stepped out of the back seat of the car.

Jeff stood next to the door, wearing his uniform and dark sunshades.

I wasn't even wearing shades because I knew Wynter didn't like them.

"Smooth landing," Jeff said.

"Agreed," I said. It better be. Even though all of Noah's pilots were the best, only the best of the best flew his family.

Of course, one of his daughters was a pilot herself, one was married to a pilot, and one was engaged to a pilot. That just left Wynter.

I'd heard rumors about Skye Travels and how Cupid tended to strike the hearts of its pilots. I didn't pay rumors any attention.

One thing about rumors, though, they had to start somewhere.

Noah had shown up unexpectedly in Birmingham yesterday to be with his wife, Savannah. While we were sitting alone in the hospital waiting room while her mother was being prepped to go home by the nurses, Savannah had confided in me that Noah had always done that for as long as she'd known him.

Even now, when they had five children together, and a happily ever after marriage, her heart still skipped when he showed up unexpectedly.

She told me that it was one of those things she liked about him, but she'd never tell him because she didn't want to encourage him.

Especially since she'd spent years training him to keep in touch with her about where he was.

So, taking a page from Noah's playbook, I decided to unexpectedly meet Wynter at the airport.

Standing at the plane's door, she froze when she saw me and I just grinned.

The surprised and pleased expression on her face was worth any trouble to track her flight and show up at just the right time.

The brisk wind blew her dark hair across her face and she shoved it aside.

With just that small movement, I was reminded just how soft her hair was.

As she stepped carefully down the steps, reaching ground, I held out a hand for her.

Smiling, she put her hand in mine.

"How are you here?" she asked me, after greeting Jeff.

"I couldn't stay away from you," I said, bending toward her, speaking for her ears only.

As I led her to the car and opened the door for her, she looked at me.

"I see you have a silver tongue," she said.

"No one's ever accused me of that before," I said, laughing.

She ducked into the seat and I closed the door.

Good God.

I'd never realized just how long three days could be.

I went around the car and slipped into the back seat next to her.

I knew I'd missed her these last three days, but I hadn't realized just how much I'd missed her until I saw her again.

She was hands down the prettiest girl I'd ever laid eyes on. Her cheeks dimpled even when she didn't know she was smiling.

But I could tell. She was smiling now, in fact, even though I was fairly certain she was trying not to.

Then she turned those bright green eyes in my direction and I knew right then and there that there would never be another girl for me.

53

WYNTER

"Where to?" Jeff asked, looking at us by the rearview mirror.

Cooper lifted a brow and looked in my direction.

"Where would you like to go?" he asked.

"You're the one who highjacked my ride," I said with a little smile. "I thought you must have a plan."

Cooper stretched out his legs and straightened his tie.

"I figured I owed you a dinner date," he said.

I knew exactly what he was talking about. He was talking about our make out session on my sister's couch in Denver.

"You don't owe me anything," I said. In fact, if anything, I felt like I owed him. I was the one who'd gotten the better side of the deal.

"Well," he said. "I guess it depends on how you look at it."

I turned the vent so that the cool air conditioning blew on my face.

The heat in my cheeks was from the hot Texas sun coming in through the window. At least that was my story. And I was sticking with it.

It wasn't from the memory of Cooper's lips on mine or the way my body responded to his hardness against me.

I turned my gaze out the window and forced myself to focus on the passing traffic.

Cooper leaned close and lowered his voice.

"At least let me buy you a drink."

I looked up in Jeff's direction and rattled off an address.

It was an upscale bar that was so close to my sister Ainsley's condo that I could walk there if I wanted to.

"Got it," Jeff said.

I relaxed against the back of the seat.

My evening had gone in a completely different direction from the way I'd expected it to.

In fact, I couldn't have imagined a better start to the evening.

I hadn't expected to see the one person I couldn't stop thinking about. I hadn't even known when I'd see him again.

In my darkest moments, it had occurred to me that he could leave Skye Travels and I'd never see him again.

To my credit, I hadn't googled him, but only because I literally hadn't had time.

Besides, I'd been afraid of what I might find.

Girlfriends. Or maybe even a wife.

But those moments had been fleeting. I was usually a pretty good judge of character. I'd certainly met enough strangers that I had developed an innate sense for that sort of thing.

But a man like Cooper would have a girlfriend. There was no way he wouldn't. He was too good looking and far, far, too good at kissing.

If any girl ever kissed him, she'd fight tooth and nail to keep him.

It was a good thing I wasn't looking for a committed relationship.

It was a good thing that I was dedicated to playing the field.

Because any girl who fell for Cooper Abrams was going to get her heart broken.

We'd talk about all this later. I wasn't interested in having a serious conversation in front of Jeff. Jeff was too much like family, but not.

Not that he was a gossip. But it would be too hard for someone to hear things and even if he didn't repeat those things, he just didn't need to know.

So I sat quietly, trying not to pay attention to how Cooper was close enough for me to reach out and touch.

That Cooper was watching me and wasn't trying to hide it.

That I couldn't stop thinking about his lips on mine.

54

COOPER

I didn't care where we went. I was content to just be sitting here next to Wynter.

She was wearing jeans and white canvas sneakers, like she'd worn the other day, but she wore a suit jacket over her black t-shirt.

I sat close enough that I could smell the fresh scent of her jasmine soap. Or maybe it was her shampoo. Whatever it was, it brought back vivid memories of the way she felt in my arms.

Jeff deftly navigated the Houston traffic. I didn't mind driving Wynter or her mother around in a car. That was odd in itself, but I didn't care much for driving on roads. I preferred to fly above it all. But I much preferred sitting here next to her.

Unable to resist not touching her any longer, I held out my hand palm up. She glanced over at me, then put her hand in mine.

I linked my fingers with hers and relaxed against the seat. This was much better.

Jeff changed lanes to drive through the EZ tag lane.

Being close to Wynter had nothing to do with sex. Not to

say that I didn't want that, but I just liked being near her. Touching her hand.

I was a man besotted, as my grandmother used to say.

It was early enough that traffic was fairly light so we reached Uptown in no time.

Then we exited 610 to the left, putting us in River Oaks. I was learning my way around Houston quick enough for a small town Alabama boy.

Jeff turned into a shopping center parking lot and went around to open Wynter's door.

I opened my own door and went around to her side.

"I'll be here when you're ready to go," Jeff said. "Take as long as you want."

I almost told him it wasn't necessary. I'd grown up driving myself and then, on my own, I'd call a taxi or an Uber. But I didn't say anything.

"Don't stay out here," Wynter told him. "Come inside."

"I will," he said with a smile. "Need to return a couple of messages first."

Apparently this was what they had worked out.

I took Wynter's hand and we walked into the bar.

Soft music played in the background and there were half a dozen people scattered about, some in booths, some at the bar.

"Where to?" I asked.

"Can we get a booth?" Wynter asked the hostess. "One of the round ones?"

"Sure thing, Miss Worthington."

It was kind of an odd thing, to me at least, walking into a bar and being recognized by name in a big city.

Shouldn't be a surprise though. The Worthington family was no doubt well-known. Much like my family was well known in three small Alabama towns. Just on a much larger scale.

We followed the hostess to a round dark blue leather booth.

Wynter slid in and around to the middle of it and I sat down next to her. She put her handbag on the other side of her.

The hostess handed us drink menus before she left us alone.

"Nice place," I said.

"It's one of my favorites," she said, shoving her menu aside without opening it.

I smiled to myself. Wynter Worthington didn't need menus.

When the server stopped at our table, Wynter ordered a martini, extra vermouth, extra olives.

I ordered a bourbon on the rocks.

"I guess the honeymoon's over," Wynter said, sipping her water.

"What do you mean?"

She looked at me with a sideways smile.

"You didn't order what I ordered."

55

WYNTER

I sipped the martini from the tall stemmed glass. They made one of the smoothest martinis I'd found in the country right here in Houston. And now that I'd traveled literally from coast to coast, I had come to the conclusion that Houston had just about the best of everything.

I was a Texan through and through.

I slid one of the tangy olives off the toothpick and watched Cooper as he studied the menu.

I didn't have to study menus. Once I'd been somewhere, I could remember two or three things from their menu that I ordered from. I didn't forget.

I considered it my hidden skill. My sister Madison's hidden skill was playing pool. Mine wasn't nearly as interesting, but I had to go with what I had. And, much like Madison with her pool playing, it was fun to have a skill most people didn't.

Cooper slid the menu aside and turned his attention to me.

I wondered what his hidden skill was. Most pilots didn't have one because they were so focused on everything airplanes.

Cooper's hidden skill was probably running a board

meeting. Not everyone could do that and certainly not too many people had a need for that skill.

"How was Denver?" he asked.

I shrugged and absently stirred my martini.

"The usual."

"Your mother tells me you're one of the best at going in and fixing companies."

"She told you that, huh?" It was an odd feeling that Cooper knew both of my parents and had had conversations with them about me.

He was getting to learn about me backwards. Learning things about me from my parents instead of from me.

It was definitely an odd feeling.

"So what else do you know about me?" I asked.

He swirled the ice in his glass as he seemed to consider.

"I know that you live at home," he said. "And you only have to look at a menu once to know what you want to order." He nodded toward the menu.

"I think you already knew those things," I said, though in truth I was pleased that he had noticed.

"You want to know what your parents told me about you," he said with a wicked little grin.

"Wouldn't you?" I asked.

He shrugged. "I really don't want to know what my parents say about me."

I laughed.

"So you say." I leaned toward him. "Are you telling me that if I went to Alabama and met your parents right now, you wouldn't care what they told me about you?"

He blew out a breath.

"You're probably right," he said.

I leaned back against my seat and slid another olive off the toothpick. The place was getting a bit crowded now.

"But there's one thing I learned that I haven't told you," he said.

"Yeah?" I met his gaze again. "What's that?"

"I learned that you've never dated a pilot."

56

COOPER

The little bar was getting crowded, but Wynter and I had one of the best seats. It was a booth, but it was round, so we were able to sit as close to each other we wanted.

And right now we were close enough that we could touch. If we wanted to.

The music playing in the background had a pleasant beat to it. One that provided a good background to the dozen or so conversations going on at once.

I usually ordered a martini, but for some reason I'd decided to order a bourbon. I think I'd just wanted to see if Wynter would notice.

And she had.

I liked it that she noticed that I hadn't ordered the same thing she had.

It meant she was paying attention to me.

Jeff came inside, saw us, then went to sit at the bar.

"He seems like a nice guy," I said, seriously trying not to be envious that he and Wynter seemed to be friendly.

"He is," Wynter said. "And he has an adorable wife. A kid on the way."

"Is that what you want?" I asked.

Wynter glanced over at me with surprise.

"You just jumped right in there with that one, didn't you?" she asked.

"Well," I said. "It seems like since I'm your boyfriend, I should know these things."

She looked at me with a slow smile and slid her last olive off her toothpick with her luscious red lips.

"Do you really want to know?" she asked.

"Of course I do. If I didn't, I wouldn't ask."

She slowly twirled her glass by the stem and looked at me from beneath her lashes.

"It's a question guys ask for a lot of reasons."

"Give me one," I said, curious now.

"It's a trick," she said. "It makes a girl think the guy is interested in a future with her." She pointed her empty toothpick at me. "It works."

"I don't understand." I picked up my share of women, but I was pretty much straight to the point. I didn't play games. I figured we both knew going into it what it was.

The music shifted into a more somber tune.

"If you're asking me if I want children," she said. "you're leading me into thinking this is going to be more than a one-night stand."

"I see." I didn't ask, but I couldn't help but wonder just how many one night stands she'd had.

If any.

I preferred to think of Wynter Worthington as being above all that.

I wanted to maintain the imagine I had in my head of her.

The one where I was the only man she looked at with those big sexy eyes and that little secret smile on her lush lips.

"Well," I said. "that's not why I'm asking."

"Then why are you asking?"

I finished off my bourbon and set the glass on the table.

"Seriously. I'm asking because as your boyfriend, I need to know what our future holds."

She was looking at me with obvious disbelief.

"Okay," she said finally.

The server stopped at our table with fresh drinks, taking our old ones.

Funny. We hadn't ordered second drinks. But Wynter seemed pleased to have more olives.

I think maybe she liked the olives better than the drink.

"Okay what?" I asked as the server left.

"Okay. I might want children. Two of them. A boy and a girl. Preferably the boy to be the oldest."

I laughed. "For a maybe, you seem to have given this a lot of thought."

"I travel a lot. Gives a girl a lot of time to think."

"I know something about that."

"I bet you do," she said. "So tell me. What's your maybe?"

57

WYNTER

*A*nother reason I loved this bar so much was that the servers kept the drinks fresh. You didn't even have to have an empty glass. They just brought you a new one after a half hour or so. I'd never actually timed it.

And I liked it that I always got extra olives without having to drink too much.

Cooper was sitting close enough that I could sway toward him just a bit and our shoulders would touch.

I didn't do it, of course. Maybe I'd do it later.

Right now, I was interested in this conversation we were having.

"I don't really have a maybe," he said. In typical male fashion, he'd just shut this conversation down.

So much for this topic.

"I have a definite," he added.

Maybe there was still hope.

"Is that so?" I asked, taking a sip of my drink. "What's your maybe?"

"Happy wife. Happy life."

I laughed. "Haven't heard that one in a while."

"Really? I just heard it."

"You're kidding, right?"

"Nope," he said, lifting his glass. "But when I heard it, it resonated with me. I knew it matched my philosophy perfectly."

"So you're saying you don't have a preference."

"About children? I'm saying my preference is whatever your preference is."

"My preference." I looked around at the young people scattered about the bar. A lot of them were younger than us, but there were some couples who were older than us, too.

Cooper was smooth. He was making me feel like he really did want to be my boyfriend.

I had a tendency to use the term loosely. He was a friend and he was a boy. Once I started kissing them, I started calling them boyfriends. Granted, I'd run a few men off with it, but that just meant they needed to go.

I'd had two guys who had taken me up on it much too easily. Would Cooper be a third?

Maybe I wanted him to.

I sipped some of my drink, before eating another olive.

"So…" I said, unable to leave it alone. "If I had told you I wanted a dozen kids, you still would have agreed with me?"

"I'd know you were lying," he said.

"How would you know that?" I asked, looking into his deep blue eyes that were closer to me than they had been a minute ago.

"Because…" he said. "You would have already gotten started."

I laughed and looked away.

"You would think," I agreed. "However, my mother started late in life. Much later. And she had five. So it's still possible."

"I'd say if you feel up to it, let's go."

My eyes widened and I swallowed.

I was a flirt. Hands down. No doubt.

But I wasn't easy. And I didn't sleep with a lot of men. Kissing. Yes. But not sex. I was far more discerning when it came to that.

"What if I said I didn't want any?" I put both my hands on the stem of my glass to keep them from trembling.

Something about this conversation had become a little too real for me.

"Then we'll use protection," I said.

There was something about the way he said it. A huskiness in his voice... that had taken this whole thing up a notch.

This was starting to feel real.

58

COOPER

Wynter had the blood rushing to my cock.

When had the talk of having children ever been a turn on for me?

Never.

But this conversation with her about how many children we each wanted had me thinking about the process of going about making those children.

As a man, I was supposed to run the other way at the first mention of children.

It's what all men did, right?

It was certainly what I had always done. I'd never had this conversation with a woman before.

Not even my high school girlfriend or my college girlfriend. We'd never gone in that direction with our conversations. And I'd dated them a couple of years.

Now here I was having this conversation with a girl I'd never even been on a date with.

We'd moved way past dating that afternoon on her sister's sofa.

This was a unique relationship.

Logically, I knew it was going too fast. Too fast and too hard.

But fast and hard was what suited Wynter.

She seemed like a straight to the point kind of girl, so there was no reason why her relationships would be any different.

I couldn't see her being coy or even playing hard to get.

Wynter Worthington didn't seem like the kind of girl who played games.

So here we were fast forwarding to the hard questions.

I decided, mostly to distract myself from my hard-on, to take it up a level.

"So now that we have a dozen... or maybe no children," I said, looking at her with a mischievous grin. "What kind of wedding do you want?"

"Wedding?" she asked, clearly not expecting this question.

I grinned. We were going at this whole thing so backwards. So backwards that instead of being wary or nervous, I was intrigued.

"Who said anything about a wedding?" she asked. Her hands were trembling.

I almost backed off, thinking I had pushed her too far.

But she seemed to get her bearings and met my gaze with a little smile of her own.

"I think an elopement should be considered," she said.

I relaxed a bit. I couldn't help it. I knew we were playing around, but I didn't know of any man who wouldn't like the idea of an elopement.

"Or maybe a big, huge church wedding," she said.

"Now you've done it," I said.

"Done what?" she asked.

I leaned forward and kissed her right on the lips.

"A big wedding," I said, pulling back ever so little. "is going to cost you a whole barrel of Yankee dimes."

She grinned and leaned forward to kiss me again.

"Everyone wins," she said. "and we all get prizes."

I kissed her again.

This girl was trouble.

In every possible way.

59

WYNTER

I wanted to jump Cooper's bones.

But good behavior was far too ingrained in me to make a scene in a public place.

It didn't matter that no one else mattered. It did matter that we weren't alone. Even Jeff, the driver was there at the bar. His presence was the most salient reminder that we weren't alone.

I pulled away from his kiss and sat back, bringing my glass to my lips. The smooth, cool glass cooled my lips, hot from his kiss.

He, too, leaned back. But he was grinning devilishly at me.

He knew what he was doing. He knew he had me turned on in every way.

So now we'd talked about how many children we wanted to have and what kind of wedding.

Part of me wanted to get out of here—to be alone with him.

And another part of me wanted to continue this titillating conversation.

I went with the delayed gratification. Only because I was afraid that if this conversation ended, we wouldn't get it back.

Since we we're actually in a relationship, I wanted to play this out for all it was worth.

"Where should we live?" I asked.

He barely missed a beat.

"We'll get our own place," he said.

"House or condo?"

"Definitely condo."

I looked at him with definite skepticism.

"What about happy wife, happy life?"

"What's the point of having a yard and all that if neither one of us is every home?"

"Good point," I said.

I agreed with him completely, but I wasn't going to tell him.

"Cats or dogs?"

"Neither," he said, then held up a hand before I could say anything. "Remember. We're never home."

"We're both going to be home with those dozen children. So… cats or dogs?"

The server stopped at our table with fresh drinks on a tray.

After he set them on our table and took our old ones away, we thanked him.

"This is a pretty cool place," Cooper said after the server walked off. "I like it."

"It's one of my favorites," I said, brushing my hair back behind my ears. It warmed my heart that Cooper liked this. One of my favorite little bars.

"We'll have to make sure to come here every week."

My heart stuttered.

"Definitely cats."

I smiled to myself.

It was too bad he wasn't a real boyfriend.

Because he was just about perfect.

60

COOPER

*W*ith nightfall, the music's beat became heavier to appeal to the younger crowd that was spilling inside.

I'd gotten a taste of Wynter's sweet lips—and it wasn't just the vodka.

She'd been right to pull away.

Kissing like that didn't belong in a public place.

I caught a glimpse of Jeff sitting alone at the bar. A young blonde woman said something to him, but he shook his head and she walked away.

The more I learned about Jeff, the more I liked him. The Worthington family was lucky to have him.

From what I'd seen, good character was a major requirement for being part of the Skye Travels family. And they were more like a family than just a company.

Noah brought his people in and made them feel like they were part of something. He'd done that for me. And I'd gotten something unexpected out of the deal.

Wynter.

I was pretty sure that had not been Noah's intent.

I was deep in thought, wondering what kind of trouble I was going to get into with Noah by kissing on his daughter when that daughter nudged my elbow.

"Hey," she said.

"Hey," I said, looking into her bright green eyes. Eyes that I could tumble into, losing myself forever.

She glanced around, then turned her gaze back to mine and leaned close.

"It's getting kind of loud in here."

I nodded. "Agreed."

"Want to get out of here?" she asked. "Go someplace else?"

"I thought you'd never ask," I said, signaling to the server for our check.

She put her glass to her lips and took a long drink. Then she turned and grinned at me as she popped the last of her olives into her mouth.

"Do you want dinner?" I asked. I didn't see how she could. She'd eaten a jar of olives.

"Okay," she said. "We can walk next door to Steak 48."

"I'll tell Jeff," I said after I paid the server for our drinks.

"Meet you up front," she said. "Need to make a restroom stop."

I made my way over to Jeff and stood next to him.

"Sorry to make you wait like this," I said.

"No need to apologize," he said. "It's just part of the job."

I nodded. I almost asked him how he tolerated the boredom, then it occurred to me that it wasn't a whole lot different from spending the day in the cockpit of an airplane. A lot of people would find that boring.

I turned and backed against the bar, waiting for Wynter.

"You and Wynter?" Jeff asked, taking a sip of his sparkling water.

"Something," I said. "Maybe."

Jeff nodded. Kept his gaze straight ahead.

"She doesn't date at home," Jeff said.

I took a minute, trying to figure out what Jeff meant by that, but he kept his gaze blank. Didn't elaborate.

"What—"

"Ready?" Wynter asked, coming up behind me.

"We'll be next door," I said to Jeff. "At the steak restaurant."

"No problem," Jeff said. "I'll be here."

"Thanks," I said.

Jeff turned to Wynter. "Just send me a text when you're ready,"

Wynter grinned and took my hand.

"Come with us," she said.

"Nah," Jeff said. "I'll be right here when you get ready to leave."

I liked Jeff just fine and knew she had to ask him to come with us. But when he said no, I was plenty relieved.

Only now his words haunted me. Words that I had no way to decipher.

She doesn't date at home.

61

WYNTER

*A*s we walked the short distance to the restaurant, Cooper's phone chimed with a text message.

He pulled his phone out of his pocket and stopped, frowning at the message.

"Everything okay?" I asked.

"Not really." He released my hand and send a quick message back.

Then his phone rang.

"I need to take this," he said. "Hello." And walked back the way we'd come.

I turned and leaned against the stone wall to wait for him.

I put my hands in my pockets and fretted about what could be wrong.

Cooper was talking to someone. Pacing.

He glanced over at me, sending my heart rate into a little bit of a flurry.

I selfishly hoped this wasn't one of those phone calls that took him away from me.

That had already happened to us once and I had been none too happy about it.

I knew we shouldn't have left our seat at the bar.

I'd been enjoying our conversation more than I'd imagined possible.

It felt almost like we'd known each other for years.

Like we really were boyfriend and girlfriend.

We weren't, of course. Just two ships passing in the night.

A couple holding hands walked down the sidewalk in front of me.

They were so into each other, they didn't even notice I was there.

That was what I wanted.

What I felt like Cooper and I could have if we were given just a chance.

But then other than him showing up at the airport today, he'd given me no indication that he was doing more than just passing the time with me.

They said it took one to know one.

I'd done my share of what they would probably call leading a man on. Not intentionally like that, but still having the same effect.

That was why I never dated near home. Whenever I got ready for a serious relationship, I'd look close to home.

My plan, however, was backfiring. I'd found a nearly perfect man right here in my own backyard.

One that I'd like to call a boyfriend for real.

And could very well be doing to me what I'd done to others. Paybacks were hell.

I needed to get my head straight.

He wasn't the first handsome man I'd enjoyed talking with.

He was just the most handsome man I'd enjoyed talking with this much.

I'd just have to push my way through it.

Cooper hung up the phone and walked back toward me.

I forced a questioning smile onto my lips.

"Good?" I asked.

"Not really," he said. "I have to go home."

My heart sank. Not just that he had to leave. But that he was still calling Alabama home.

Would he ever feel like this was his home? Or was he one of those people who always saw their hometown as home?

Probably the latter and I would probably be the same way if I were in his shoes.

I didn't blame him for it.

But right now I needed to go into psychologist mode.

"Tell me what's wrong," I said, taking the hands of my new boyfriend and looking into his eyes.

62

COOPER

*W*ynter took both my hands and looked into my eyes.

I knew I couldn't hide the pain from her, so I didn't even try.

"It's my father," I said, swallowing thickly.

She waited, squeezing my hands firmly.

"He's having emergency surgery in Birmingham," I said, the words sinking in as I said them out loud.

Pulling one hand free, I ran it through my hair and pressed my palm against my forehead.

"What's happened?" she asked.

"That was my mom," I said. "The service was bad, but… she told me to come home."

I couldn't get my thoughts to settle.

Traffic raced past on Westheimer Street. A couple, laughing, walked past us on the sidewalk.

I'd just seen my father. He was fine. Never sick a day in his life.

Wynter pulled out her phone and was calling someone.

"Daddy," she said. "Cooper needs to get to… hold on." She looked at me. "Birmingham, right?"

"Right," I said.

"He needs to get to Birmingham," she said. "A family emergency."

She waited a beat.

"Yes," she said, looking at me. "Tonight."

I nodded.

I heard Noah's voice but couldn't make out his words.

"Yes," she said. Then she put him on speaker and sent a message.

"I'll get the flight plan filed," Noah said. "Tell him to head to the airport."

"Got it," she said. "Thanks Daddy."

By the time she hung up the phone, Jeff walked out of the bar and headed straight for the car.

"Come on," she said, pulling me toward the parking lot where Jeff was already backing out.

We slid into the back seat and Wynter was back on her phone. Texting.

"You have a flight scheduled to leave in one hour," she said.

"That was fast." I couldn't say how happy I was that she was the one making the plans. For the first time in my life, I felt completely helpless and out of sorts.

"Do you need anything else?" she asked. "Clothes?"

Did I?

"No," I said. "I have clothes there."

She nodded and clasped her fingers in mine.

I might be sick. This was hands down THE worst feeling I had ever had.

I didn't know how to do this. I didn't know how to face one of the worst things a child had to face in their lifetimes.

Why did it have to be now?

Just when things were going so well. New job. I pulled

Wynter closer and nestled her head against my chest. New girlfriend.

I needed to call one of my brothers. Or one of my sisters. Or call my mother back. But everyone was probably making their own way to the hospital. I didn't know who all was there.

My grandfather would need to get here and I was one who would need to fly him to Alabama, but I was trying to get myself there.

I ran my fingers through Wynter's hair.

I could do this.

As long as she was with me.

And that could be a problem.

"Come with me," I said.

63

WYNTER

"What?" I asked. Surely I heard him wrong.

"Come with me," he said again.

I had heard him right.

I lifted my head to look up at him — into his clear blue eyes. Eyes full of pain. And... something else.

"To Alabama?" I asked.

"Why not?" he asked. "You can meet my family."

I hadn't been expecting this. Not in a million years.

"But... Really?... Why?"

"I can't get enough of you." He hugged me close and whispered in my ear.

I looked at him with all sorts of skepticism. But my heart did summersaults.

I mentally reviewed my schedule. I'd just gotten home from a job in Denver. I clicked open my phone. Opened my calendar.

I had three days off before my next job. And if I needed to, I could consult with them via Zoom. It was a small job. Smaller than usual, but I'd worked with them before.

It was a job in Memphis, so it wasn't that far off from here or Birmingham. I could still get there from Birmingham if I needed to without too much trouble.

My thoughts raced in about fifty different directions.

Instead of answering, I leaned back against Cooper's chest and closed my eyes.

Going with him took things to a whole different level. Sure, he'd met my family, but my family was work related. Meeting his family was straight up personal.

Jeff was on the car phone, talking to someone at Skye Travels.

It sounded halfway personal, so I tried not to listen.

It would have been hard for me to hear, anyway, over the pounding blood in my ears.

Cooper ran a hand along my arm, whether to soothe himself or me, I didn't know. Probably a win-win.

We turned into Skye Travels parking lot and we all climbed out of the car.

A gust of wind blew my hair into my eyes.

Cooper took my hand and we went straight through the gate.

The small jet, the Skye Travels logo splashed in red across the tail, stood ready and waiting.

Daddy came walking around from the back of the plane. Looking at me. Then looked at Cooper and back again.

"Ready to go?" he asked Cooper.

Cooper nodded, then looked at me.

Squeezing my hand, he kissed my cheek.

My heart went out to him. Then as he walked away, my heart nearly broke.

He was the closest thing to a boyfriend I'd had since I was in high school.

Cooper slung his leather computer bag over his shoulder as he walked toward the plane.

He should have been the pilot. And even though I still hadn't flown with him, I'd ridden with him in cars.

So strange.

"Wait," I said.

Cooper stopped and turned around. He and Daddy both stood there looking at us.

"I'm going with you."

64

COOPER

*U*nder any other circumstances, I would been in the cockpit next to Noah Worthington. The man was a legend in the world of aviation.

The chance to fly with him was an unanticipated bonus to working at Skye Travels. One I'd sacrificed without a second thought.

There would be other opportunities to sit in a cockpit with Noah. Right now all I wanted to do was to sit next to Wynter.

Noah got in the plane into the air without a hitch.

But in this particular case, I sat in the back next to Wynter, our hands linked.

Just as the plane was taking off, I got a text message from my mother that they were taking my father in for surgery.

My return text, asking what kind of surgery, sat there undelivered and unanswered.

I was used to this way of life. Of not having service in the air. But it was different now. I had so many unanswered questions. Questions that wouldn't be answered until we landed.

When I'd asked Wynter to come with me, I hadn't expected her to actually do it.

Now I had her with me. And oddly enough, she had her luggage with her. She hadn't gone home yet since landing from Denver.

"Are you okay?" she asked, squeezing my hand.

I took a deep breath. I was better with her here than I would have been if she wasn't.

That was one thing I was certain of.

"My father is a strong man," I said. "Never sick a day in his life. He'll be okay."

Maybe if I said it out loud, I would believe and maybe it would come true.

Putting positive vibes in the air never hurt anything. Hurt a lot less than putting out negative vibes.

She put her other hand over our clasped hands.

"Whatever you need," she said. "Just tell me."

I looked at her. Just looked at her.

She was beautiful. The clearest pale skin. Little dimples in her cheeks that were obvious when she smiled and just the shadow of dimples when she thought about smiling.

Her dark, smooth as silk hair touched her shoulders, curving in places on the ends. She tucked a stray strand behind her ear and looked at me questioningly.

Her plush bee-stung lips, curving into a perfect cupid's bow, begged to be kissed, especially with the natural positive upturn at the corners.

Her eyes, framed with dark thick lashes, wore a sweep of sparkly bronze shadow across her lids.

She was perfect.

And it wasn't just that she was sexy as hell. She was kind and funny and intelligent. I couldn't remember the last time I'd enjoyed a conversation as much as I enjoyed my conversations with her.

"How about a Yankee Dime?" I asked.

She smiled. A slow, mysterious smile.

Then she closed her eyes and leaned towards me.

65

WYNTER

I didn't consider myself to be impulsive.

Spontaneous at times, but not impulsive.

Thinking about the difference in this situation was, perhaps, splitting hairs.

With nothing but air beneath us and the deep roar of the plane motor around us, my lips touched Cooper's.

As we flew through the darkness, he deepened the kiss.

Kissing him while Daddy piloted the plane felt deliciously risqué. Even though my family owned the largest private airline in the country and I'd grown up in the world of aviation, I had never, not once, kissed anyone while in flight.

Doing so brought a whole new perspective to my world.

Was this how Madison and Kade had fallen in love? My parents?

It was possible. And it gave me a new understanding of what their lives might be like.

Cooper had said he couldn't get enough of me.

The feeling was mutual.

I couldn't get enough of him.

So much so that I had hopped a plane with him.

My reasons though were not that I was smitten by him—though I was. My reason was to go as a supportive friend.

A girlfriend.

Friends didn't kiss like this. Not even in my flirty world. A world where I rarely went to a different city without finding someone to kiss.

It wasn't my fault that I like kissing and guys liked kissing me.

But right now I couldn't think of a single one of them. Everyone else faded in Cooper's shadow.

We hit a pocket of air and I straightened, my lips separating from his.

I smiled at him and looked into his eyes. Eyes that reflected my own passion. I knew that look. That look told me that it was time to back off. That he wanted more than kissing.

This look was where I became discerning and rarely let things progress. I considered it my own code of morality.

Right now, though, I wasn't sure I wanted him to stop.

In fact, it was probably a good thing we were on this airplane, strapped into our seats. Otherwise, all bets were off.

He swept his thumb across my bottom lip and my eyes drifted closed.

I was glad I'd broken my own rule. Maybe Never Kiss a Pilot should now be Only Kiss this Pilot.

I smiled at the thought.

I was in a heap of trouble when it came to Cooper Abrams.

A kind of trouble I rarely let myself get to. I was a flirt with 'em and leave 'em kind of girl.

But Cooper did not fit into that category.

Cooper didn't fit into any of my categories.

He was something new and different.

He was a man I actually wanted to keep.

I bit my bottom lip as I wondered how Elise had possibly seen that in our kitchen the very first day I'd met Cooper.

66

COOPER

*A*s the wheels hit the runway in Birmingham, reality came crashing back along with a barrage of text messages.

I scrolled though, looking for information on my father's condition, but all I got was a host of updates on my family's whereabouts. I also got a confirmation that he was at UAB, something I already assumed.

While I was on my phone, Wynter was on hers.

"We have a car waiting," she said.

"Already?" I asked, only halfway paying attention.

"Are you kidding? This is my mother's old stomping ground. Skye Travels is a regular."

"Right," I said, suddenly putting it together. Wynter would be quite familiar with Birmingham since her grandmother still lived here.

Since I wasn't actually from Birmingham, but a small town about an hour away, I hadn't really made the connection until now.

Wynter had family here. That was as good an explanation as any why she had agreed to come with me.

The realization took a little bit of the wind out of my sails, but it didn't change the way she smiled at me.

She smiled at me like a girlfriend would.

We'd gone from total strangers to being completely comfortable around each other in a New York minute. Maybe that was how it worked when something was right.

And being with Wynter felt right in every possible way.

"Any updates?" she asked.

"Not really." I shook my head. "Just that he's a UAB, but I already figured that."

"It's not far," she said. "We're almost there."

I hated seeing the compassion in her eyes. Not that hated her being compassionate, but because seeing her concern made things seem more real.

I wished we were coming here to visit my family under happy circumstances.

"Are you planning to stay with your grandmother?" I asked.

Her response was mixture of surprise and hurt.

"I don't know," she said. "If you want me to."

The conversation was interrupted by my phone ringing.

"Hello," I said, keeping my gaze on Wynter's for strength, even as my heart was terrified that this phone call was bad news.

"Are you here?" It was my older brother on the line. "They're bringing Father out of surgery."

"Just landed," I said.

"Good," he said. "See you shortly."

Then he hung up without even saying good-bye.

I stared at my phone for a second.

"We're almost there," Wynter said.

I just nodded.

Even though I knew that Wynter might be staying with her family, I hoped she wouldn't. I hoped she would stay with me.

It didn't seem like too much to ask.

I took both her hands and kissed the backs of her fingers.

"Stay with me," I whispered.

"Of course," she said, unbuckling her belt.

Then she wrapped her arms around me and I got lost in the feel of her in my arms.

67

WYNTER

The next few minutes were a whirlwind.

We deplaned and Cooper helped the driver put my luggage in the car.

"I'm going to visit your grandmother," Daddy said as we stood next to the airplane.

"Okay," I said. "I'm going with Cooper."

"I thought you would," Daddy said with a little grin. "I'll call you after a bit. Before I fly out. Just in case."

"I understand," I said. "Thank you.

I gave Daddy a quick hug, then walked to where Cooper waited next to the car.

The lights around the tarmac warded off the darkness. The scent of jet fuel was familiar and comforting.

Cooper nodded at Daddy as he opened the car door for me and I slipped inside.

I couldn't help but wonder what Daddy was thinking. One of my sisters had already married a pilot and another was engaged to one. My other sister, Ainsley, was a pilot herself, but even her husband was a pilot.

We were a family of pilots.

And psychologists.

Daddy didn't know that I had a rule against crushing on pilots. Even if he did, I was fairly certain he would understand.

These things happened.

Cooper and I rode in silence, our hands laced together.

The driver pulled up to the hospital door and took my luggage out of the car while Cooper held my door.

He was looking over his shoulder toward the doors.

"Go ahead," I said, stepping out of the car.

"What are you going to do with your luggage?" he asked.

"I'll figure something out," I said, shooing him away. "Go."

I knew what it was like to be worried about someone in the hospital. Daddy had gone through a bout with cancer. I'd been there.

He looked at me with uncertainty.

"I'll find you," I said.

Finally, he turned and sprinted inside the doors.

I sighed.

The chauffeur helped me get my luggage inside and took it to a locked storage room. I'd only brought one suitcase with me. I'd sent the others home with Daddy. This was the only one with all clean clothes anyway.

The driver left and I was alone.

"I'm looking for Mr. Abrams," I told the receptionist.

She gave me directions to the surgical waiting area and I headed in that direction.

I wiped my palms on my jeans. I was about to meet Cooper's family. His mother and probably his siblings. And it wasn't like I was meeting them during ordinary circumstances.

I was meeting them during a very difficult and stressful time.

They would probably be none too happy to see me under these circumstances.

My mother would have been welcoming. I'd never seen her

otherwise. Fortunately, no one had brought any unannounced visitors to test that out.

I stopped at the door to the waiting room and looked inside.

I hadn't seen this many people together in one family room since Daddy had been in the hospital.

In fact, I immediately flashed back to when Daddy had surgery back in Houston. The waiting room had been bigger, but not private like this. This room was furnished in about the same way. Comfortable couches and a big television on the wall. The television was off and the room was quiet, except for the overhead announcements that drifted in from the hallways.

I immediately spotted a woman who had to be Mrs. Abrams. She was a dignified looking lady wearing a deep emerald skirt and jacket…about my mother's age.

Cooper was sitting next to her, but the dozen or so other people in the room were either sitting or standing around talking in hushed tones. They all wore worried expressions and I saw lots of knitted brows.

It could have easily been my own family.

Cooper looked up and saw me standing there.

"Mother," he said. "My girlfriend's here."

Everyone else must have heard him, too, because the whole room went quiet.

68

COOPER

I was, of course, the last one to arrive, though not by much. My siblings had all driven in to Birmingham. Wynter had been so quick to get my flight arranged that my arrival wasn't even noticeably behind those who had driven their cars.

I'd been to this hospital before, but never in one of these waiting rooms. It was obviously designed to give the illusion of not being a waiting room in a hospital. No plastic chairs or magazines on the end tables.

Instead, there was a bookcase on one wall filled with a couple dozen paperbacks. Nice touch. There was a charging station at a little desk on another wall. A compact little kitchen area with a refrigerator and coffee station filled the far right corner.

Despite what was designed to be comfortable surroundings, the room felt cold to me. Cold and sterile. No matter how much they tried to disguise it.

But when I saw Wynter standing at the door, much of that coldness vanished.

Everyone turned to look at her expectantly, probably looking for news about Father.

But now that I'd announced her as my girlfriend, the looks changed to skepticism.

I wasn't surprised about that. I hadn't brought a girl home since high school and then to bring a girl home when my father was having emergency surgery... They had every right to be surprised.

But I didn't care. I wanted everyone to know about Wynter. I wanted to shout it from the rooftops.

She was looking a bit pale... maybe it was from the lighting. Or maybe it was from walking into a room of not just strangers, but my family.

There were a lot of us. And no one was feeling all that receptive.

But I hadn't chosen the timing. The timing had chosen us.

So they would all just have to deal with it. Or not. I didn't care.

As I took her hand in mine, the doctor turned the corner and stepped into the room.

Although he was a stranger to me, my first impression was that he looked tired.

He spotted Mother and went to stand in front of her.

"These all family members?" he asked.

"Yes." Mother stood up and faced him directly.

I saw her jaw clench as she braced herself.

"Mr. Abrams came through the surgery just fine."

There was a collective sigh across the room and everyone visibly relaxed.

"He'll have to start doing daily exercises and incorporate more whole foods into his diet from here on out."

The doctor continued, but whatever he was saying would no doubt have to be repeated.

"When can I see him?" Mother asked, interrupting the doctor's instructions.

The doctor glanced around the room.

"Give him a couple of hours to wake up, then you can see. But just you right now."

I squeezed Wynter's hand and she smiled at me.

I had questions. So many questions. But they could wait.

As the doctor left, my mother sat back down in the chair and closed her eyes.

Now was certainly not the time to introduce Wynter to the family.

69

WYNTER

"*L*et's go get some coffee," Cooper said.

There was a coffee station in the corner, but I knew what Cooper was saying.

He was saying he wanted to get out of here. To get away from his family.

I certainly wasn't going to argue. I felt like an intruder. And it wasn't the right time for him to be introducing anyone, not even a new girlfriend.

Everyone was focused on Mr. Abrams' condition. As they should be.

He took my hand and linked our fingers together as we left the waiting room and walked down the deserted hallway toward the elevator.

A young male nurse dressed in scrubs got on the elevator with us, standing in front of us as the elevator went down.

Cooper and I looked at each other. His blue eyes sparkled as he looked at me.

The sparkle was coming back in his eyes as relief settled over him.

I much preferred it to the worry and anxiety that had been on his features the last few hours.

The elevator doors opened and the nurse stepped off, hurrying off to do whatever he'd been called to do.

Cooper and I stepped off together and walked toward the little hospital café.

"You want coffee?" he asked.

"Sure," I said, ignoring the hunger pangs that reminded me I hadn't had anything to eat other than olives since lunch which was hours ago. In Denver actually and now I was in Alabama.

I traveled a lot compared to most people, but I couldn't ever remember having lunch in one state, drinks in another, and coffee in a third. Only in airports. Not off the plane in town.

We both made lattes in one of the coffee machines and went to the checkout counter.

It was odd how the coffee machine was state of the art, but they still had a person sitting at a register. It was only a matter of time before the checker's job was obsolete.

"Lordy mercy," the woman said with a big, toothy grin. She was about our age, but somehow she'd looked older in the plain brown uniform.

"Cooper Abrams," she said. "Is that you?"

"It's me," Cooper said, pulling out his credit card and sliding it through the machine.

"How are you Emma?" he asked.

Emma leaned forward and lowered her voice. "Just got myself divorced from that no good son-of-a-bitch Johnny Martin." She glanced at me. "Pardon my French."

I shrugged and picked up my coffee. "I've heard worse," I said.

"I didn't know you'd married him," Cooper said. "But I guess I should have known after all those years you two dated."

"Well," Emma said, looking at me again. "Just 'cause they're popular football players in high school don't mean they're gonna turn out to be husbands."

"Don't I know it," I said. Not that I had any personal experience. I'd never dated a football player.

Emma grinned.

"Cooper," she said. "You did good for yourself. Hold on to this one."

"I will," Cooper said as we turned and walked toward a table.

"Tell your daddy I hope he feels better," Emma called behind us.

"Will do," Cooper said over his shoulder.

We sat at a little table out of earshot of Emma.

"Only in Alabama, huh?" he said.

"Oh no," I said. "It's everywhere."

I sipped the hot coffee.

"But she's right about one thing," I said, with a little wink.

"What's that?" he asked. "Never marry a football player?"

"No," I said, glancing over my shoulder at Emma. "You better hold onto this one."

70

COOPER

*I*t was odd being back here in Birmingham. I'd gone to private school here in the city for the last two years of high school, so people knew me not only in my small home town, but also here in Birmingham, mostly the people I'd gone to school with.

I had a vague memory of Emma, though to be honest, I hadn't given her any thought. She wasn't my type.

As for what my type was, she was sitting right in front of me.

And the funny thing was, I didn't even know that until Wynter had walked into my life. I guess technically I had walked into hers.

"As soon as I talk you into an elopement, we'll nail this thing down."

I laughed, nearly spitting out my coffee."

"You asked for it," I said with a grin.

"I think if your family is anything like mine, we'd both be in too much trouble to ever live that down."

"You're probably right," I said, in truth the thought of having a big wedding with the Worthingtons and the Abrams left me feeling a bit unsettled.

"But the thought of our two families together is a little overwhelming, isn't it?" she asked.

Leaning back, I took a big gulp of coffee, then looking into her eyes, I shook my head.

"What?"

"Wynter Worthington," I said. "You might just be the perfect woman."

She grinned at me, then nodded over my shoulder. "I think someone might be looking for you."

I turned around. My older brother Bradford was walking toward us, coffee cup in hand.

Without asking for permission, he slid out a chair with his right foot and sat down between us.

That's what happened when a guy grew up knowing his destiny was to run an empire of family run banks. To my knowledge, my brother had never, not once, had his power questioned.

The guy had never even been on a job interview. Thirty-five years old and not a day of rejection in his blood.

Couldn't help but wonder what that would be like.

Wynter sipped her coffee, biding her time, probably waiting to see how we would interact.

I would imagine that a psychologist would be curious about my family.

A girlfriend would be curious, too.

And a psychologist girlfriend... well...

"I'm Bradford," my brother said, looking at Wynter.

Wynter leaned forward, leaning her elbows on the table.

"I'm Wynter Worthington," she said.

My brother crossed his arms, sat back, and looked at me.

A slow smiled spread across his face.

"Seriously?" he asked.

I knew what my brother was asking. That one word was his

way of saying *Are you seriously dating the boss's daughter? I thought you knew better than to do something like that.*

My fingers wrapped around my paper coffee cup, I looked into Wynter's eyes.

"Seriously."

71

WYNTER

I knew men like Bradford Abrams. I worked with them all the time.

They were powerful men. Men who thought they owned the world. When in fact, they actually did. They owned their little part of the world. Big fish in a little pond.

I wasn't intimidated.

I'd grown up around big fish in big ponds. People were just people.

It was hard to fathom how Cooper had come from this world.

Cooper didn't seem anything like Bradford's type.

Cooper had taken a job with Skye Travels that had led him to do all sorts of thing like chauffeur me around. I couldn't even imagine Bradford doing that.

"How's your father?" I asked Bradford.

He must be here for some reason unless of course he'd stopped by to torture his brother about his new girlfriend.

"Made it through the surgery," Bradford said. "Now we wait and see."

"Mother will be better after she sees him," Cooper said. "We all will."

"Have you heard from Gramps?" Bradford asked.

"No," Cooper said, pulling his phone out of his pocket and scrolling through his messages. "Nothing."

"He chartered a flight home."

"Who with?" Cooper asked.

Bradford shrugged. "I don't know. My assistant set it up."

"Is somebody picking him up at the airport at least?"

"We'll get somebody there, I'm sure."

Bradford didn't seem to have a whole lot of concern about much of anything and to be honest, that had been my first impression of Cooper with his dark shades. Men in dark sunshades always seem to wear an air of arrogance. Just my own personal bias.

At any rate, I wasn't willing to jump to conclusions about Cooper's brother.

The family was under a whole lot of stress and it wasn't fair to make assumptions about someone when they were under that kind of stress.

"Well," Bradford said, scooting back his chair and standing up. "I need to head out."

"You're leaving?" Cooper asked.

"Got a meeting," he said.

We both watched as Bradford walked out of the café.

I turned to Cooper. Started to make a comment about his brother. Instead I decided to change the subject.

"Did you find out what kind of surgery your father had?"

"His heart," Cooper said. "They didn't have time to get him to Atlanta."

"His heart," I said. "Wow. I guess you'll find out more about it."

"I will," he said. "but I wanted to give my mother time to see him first."

"Your parents?" I wrapped my hands around the coffee cup and straightened the cardboard sleeve. A zarf they called it. "They're close?"

"Oh my God," he sat back, ran a hand through his hair. "Are they. They met in high school and have been together ever since. I don't think either one of them can imagine a life without the other. I know I can't."

I smiled at him. He'd just unknowingly given me a whole lot of information about himself.

Children who were raised with parents who were in loving marriages tended to have long term meaningful relationships as well. But I wouldn't tell him that. I didn't want him to think that I was trying to be in a long-term relationship with him.

But was I?

I'd have to think about that later.

"I'm so glad he came through it okay," I said.

He held out his hand, palm up, and I put my hand in his.

This. This was more than I had hoped for.

And with him it had come unexpectedly.

But didn't it always?

72

COOPER

We worked out shifts for staying with my father.

I sat next to his bed in a private room, of course, which looked more like a hotel room than a hospital room. That is if you could tune out the regular beeping of the monitors and the nurses coming in and out. Then there was also the IV stuck in his arm.

Minor details that provided a constant reminder that this was a hospital room.

And add to that the fact that he hadn't been awake yet. My mother said he opened his eyes once while she was with him, but he'd been incoherent.

My shift fell into the middle of the night.

I think my brother, Bradford, who set the whole thing up, did that on purpose.

Why he decided to mess with me, I don't know.

Probably because I hadn't told him about Wynter until just showing up out of the blue with her. What he would never understand was that there had been nothing to tell until now.

And to be quite honest I didn't really know if there really was anything to tell.

I didn't know if we really had anything or if we were just playing a game.

If it was a game, it felt incredibly real. Too real for comfort.

What I did know was that it wasn't a game for me.

For me it was about as real as it got.

And how that happened at all, much less so damn quick, I couldn't say.

Wynter was the perfect woman.

How I'd stumbled over her at this point in my life would forever be a mystery.

I wasn't a playboy, not exactly. I just hadn't found anyone that I wanted to be in a committed relationship with. In as long as I could remember.

Father opened his eyes.

"Cooper?" His voice was raspy and low.

Seeing my father like this cut me to the quick.

I wasn't ready to see my parents like this. They were still young and energetic. At least they had been until now.

I scooted forward in the chair.

"Father." The word caught in my throat and I swallowed down the wave of emotion that came over me. I had to be strong. For him.

I could have my existential crisis later. When I was alone. That's what flying time was for. Just me and airplane and the clouds. The world below.

The thoughts that I had in the cockpit stayed in the cockpit.

"How do you feel?" I asked, putting my hand on his arm.

Father closed his eyes again, then opened them and looked at me.

"Like hell."

I laughed, and some of the tension dissipated.

"I know you do."

"So they left you with me?" He grimaced and tried to lift his arm, then thought better of it.

"It's my shift," I said. "Bradford made the schedule."

"Bradford. Something's going on with him."

"What is it?"

"Hell if I know," Father said. "He isn't talking to me about it."

"Well, whatever it is, I hope he gets over it."

"You and me both."

We sat in silence for a few minutes.

The beeping of the monitors filling the emptiness.

"So am I going to live?" he asked.

"Yes, Father. You're going to live."

"Who's going to tell me what the hell happened?"

A nurse came into the room right then.

"I think this nurse is the one who can tell you that."

"Welcome back," the nurse, Anna said.

"My boy seems to think I'm going to live."

"There was never any doubt about that, Mr. Abrams," Anna said, checking his fluids.

I sat back in my chair and let the relief wash over me.

I hadn't known just how worried I'd been until this moment.

Father would be back on his feet in no time.

And I would be able to go back to work.

I never thought I'd find a job I liked better than flying.

But being Wynter's pilot and her chauffeur was a job custom created just for me.

I was getting paid to do the thing that I would have done for nothing.

That was a true sign of a perfect job.

73

WYNTER

I opened my suitcase and sorted through the clothes inside. I literally had nothing more than business clothes.

I'd ended up wearing all my casual clothes at the job site in Denver. I'd had to in order to fit into the work culture.

So as a result, I would be wearing work clothes here while I was visiting with Cooper.

It wasn't necessarily a bad thing.

His sisters had worn pants suits. So my skirts and jackets weren't going to be so off-base as they could have been.

I hadn't even brought my jeans and other casual clothes. Just the ones I happened to have been wearing today.

Dropping the lid on my suitcase, I looked around the bedroom.

The Abram's house was unpretentious. It was different from my father's house in that it looked more lived in.

Momma hated clutter and knickknacks. She barely even had pictures on the walls.

She said it was important to *rest her eyes.*

I think that's where my sister Brianna got it. Brianna had a

You Tube channel, a very popular channel, where she talked about the benefits of minimalism.

It didn't bother me one way or the other really. I didn't keep a lot of stuff around, but I didn't make a big deal out of it.

Living at home, all I had to worry about was my own bedroom, so I had yet to have my own place. Living a large percentage of my life in hotel rooms sort of made that choice for me.

I had to admit that living in hotel rooms was getting a bit tedious. I found myself imagining what kind of place I'd like to live if I lived by myself.

Though right now I was actually thinking about what kind of place Cooper and I would live in.

That was a dangerous direction.

Just because I was here spending the night in his parents' house didn't mean that we were actually in a committed relationship headed toward living together or more.

I stood up straight and took a deep breath.

Bradford had dropped me and Mrs. Abrams off, then left for his own house.

Mrs. Abrams had apologized for not being a good hostess and excused herself. She had to be exhausted. The emotional toll required to get her through today had been enough to leave anyone exhausted.

I was exhausted and Mr. Abrams was a stranger to me.

But his son...

His son was another matter entirely.

His family was big like mine, but I didn't know if they were anything like the Worthingtons.

The Worthingtons were friendly and welcoming. I had to give the Abrams a chance. A chance to get past this crisis in their lives.

Then. Then maybe they would be more like my family.

They were certainly bigger by a bit.

But not as spread out. They all lived within the Birmingham area. Three different directions though.

I was fortunate that out of all my siblings only one of them lived in another state. The rest of us were all in Houston.

I slipped out of my skirt and put on a t-shirt.

The bed was huge for a guest room—a king bed. Fortunately I was used to sleeping in strange places so I could sleep just about any place.

Maybe I should have gotten a hotel room. Actually I'd already agreed to stay here before I found out Cooper wasn't going to be here.

Now I was in a strange place—not a problem in itself—but I didn't have a driver. Would it be rude to call an Uber in the morning to take me to Starbuck's for coffee and a biscuit?

Normally I wouldn't care, but Cooper had gone and introduced me as his girlfriend.

Well hell.

Paybacks for any of the guys I'd introduced as my boyfriend over the years.

I'd just have to deal with this in the morning.

I'd gotten myself into it. I'd get myself out.

74

COOPER

I ended up taking an Uber to my parents' house after my youngest sister showed up an hour later than she had been scheduled for.

Wynter had gone with my mother and I couldn't think of more nerve-wracking situation than that.

No telling what Mother would tell Wynter.

And I'd barely even had the chance to introduce them.

Guess that's how she felt with me talking to her parents when I first met her.

It was disconcerting at best.

I walked through the front door of the house I'd grown up in.

It had been and still was a comfortable home. Lots of open space. Lots of places to sit. Couches. Chairs. A huge dining room table.

And on the few occasions we were all together, people spill out of the dining room and had to sit in the living room on one of the two large couches.

I rarely came home for those gatherings anymore. I'd distanced myself from all that after I'd left for college.

I didn't want the inconvenience. Well that was biting me in the butt now.

My father had nearly died and I'd hardly spent any time with him in years. The only time we spent together had something to do with business.

Sitting in the hospital room together was the first time we'd sat in a room together and not talked business since as far back as I could remember.

That's how it went, though, right? Adult children were supposed to grow up and move off. They were supposed to become part of their wife's family.

Did it matter that I was thirty years old and didn't have a wife?

At five in the morning, the house was quiet. It was kinda eerie because my father always… always…got up at four thirty every morning, sat at the breakfast nook, and read the Wall Street Journal, the New York Times, and the local paper. All that before heading out to work. He had always been the first one to get to the bank and was the last one to leave.

And look where it had gotten him.

In the hospital fighting for his life.

I set my keys and wallet on the breakfast table where my father was supposed to be sitting.

There had to be more to life than reading newspapers and being the first one to show up for work.

There had to be. I'd never wanted to live my life like that and I wasn't going to start now.

Life was too damn short not to live it to the fullest. Every. Single. Day.

I went over to the coffee machine. The same old-fashioned machine they'd had for years… and started a pot of coffee.

The ground coffee was still in the same place where it had always been.

For my father to spend so much of his life trying to make

money and being around money all day long every single day, he surely didn't know how to spend it.

Would this be a wake-up call for him?

Would he take Mother on that cruise they'd been talking about for years instead of calling a trip to Alaska to visit Grandpa a vacation?

That wasn't a vacation. A vacation was getting away together. Just the two of them. Someplace they wanted to go. Not someplace they were obligated to go for family or business.

As I stood staring at the coffee slowly dripping into the pot, I felt someone watching me from behind.

I was pretty sure it wasn't my mother. She never got up this early and even if she did, she would have said something. As far as I knew there was no one else in the house. Except for Wynter.

My heart beating quickly, I turned around.

She stood there in the doorway, looking uncertain. She was wearing a long baggy t-shirt and a pair of pajama bottoms in a cute little teddy bear print.

Her hair hung loose, like it always did, but it looked different. Like sleepy bed hair.

"Hi," she said, rubbing her arms.

"Good morning," I said. "Coffee?"

I couldn't pull my gaze away from her. She was utterly and completely adorable.

"Yes," she said, but neither one of us moved.

I kicked at my brain cells, trying to get them in gear.

"You're up early," I said.

"Bad habit," she said with a shrug.

The coffee machine beeped, telling me the coffee was ready.

"You and my father sound like kindred spirits."

"How is he?" she asked, her brows knitted.

"Good," I said. "He was awake when I left."

"That's great news," she said. "You must be relieved."

"I am."

She shifted from one foot to the other.

"Coffee?" she asked.

"Coffee," I said, remembering that I'd offered her coffee. "Right."

I turned and took two solid white mugs from the cabinet.

"I thought about calling an Uber to take me to Starbuck's," she said, coming around the kitchen island to stand next to me.

"Seriously?" I glanced over at her.

"It's a habit." She shrugged. "When I travel I go to Starbucks."

I poured coffee into the two mugs.

"What do you order?"

"Vanilla latte. Skinny. Extra vanilla. Extra hot." She rattled off her order like she'd done it a thousand times. "One of those biscuit things, too."

I opened the refrigerator. Found a bottle of creamer.

"I don't think they have a frother," I said.

She smiled and held out her hand for the bottle.

"It's okay. I can make do."

She poured creamer into her coffee and put the bottle back into the refrigerator.

I didn't want her to have to make do. I wanted everything to be perfect for her.

She held up her mug, then took a sip.

"Not bad," she said with a little smile, but I didn't miss the way her nose crunched up just a little bit.

I took the mug from her hands and set it on the counter.

"What?" she asked. "It's good."

"I want to show you how we should start the day," I said, pulling her close and wrapping my arms around her.

She felt so good. So soft. So warm.

I put a hand beneath her chin and tilted her face up just enough that I could look at her.

Her eyes were closed and her lips were parted just a little.

With a groan, I lowered my lips to hers. She tasted like coffee and vanilla creamer. She tasted like a latte.

And I couldn't get enough of her.

I picked her up by the waist and set her on the kitchen island behind her.

Pulling her bottom close to the edge, against my pelvis. My God. She fit perfectly against me. It's like she was made for me.

With a groan, I ground my lips against her.

I couldn't get enough of her.

75

WYNTER

I laced my fingers in Cooper's silky, short hair and surrendered to him, my senses overwhelmed.

He was everywhere. His tongue caressed mine while his lips caressed my lips.

My legs were wrapped around him and his hands were on my bottom, keeping me close dangerously close to the edge of the counter. His hardness pressed against that special soft place that was sensitive to every touch.

When I didn't think he could get any closer to me, he did. Our bodies melded together until we were indistinguishable. I couldn't tell where I stopped and he started.

Then the pressure started to build and I gasped.

I pushed my hips toward him, moving in little circles. His hands were holding me up and I was pretty sure my legs were wrapped around him and I wasn't sitting on the counter anymore.

The dangerousness of it all sent the blood rushing toward my soft spot.

I dug into his shoulders with fingertips, hanging onto him

for dear life while letting go of any control I might have had at the same time.

God help me. I was going to come. My mind went blank and the sensations rushed through every cell of my being.

My lips left his and pressed my chin against his shoulder.

I gulped for air and went limp against him.

I felt the counter firmly beneath my bottom again as I started to come back to reality.

I let out a deep sigh and a smile spread across my lips.

This was getting to be a habit. And it was a habit I could most definitely get used to.

He held me close, pressing his fingertips into my back, massaging my muscles. An orgasm and a massage all in one.

I couldn't think of a better way to start the day.

"You know what," he said.

"What?" I murmured against his shoulder.

"I'm thinking a trip to Starbuck's isn't such a bad idea after all."

"I'm not dressed," I said, with a little bubble of laughter.

"You look to me like you're wearing far too many clothes."

I felt the heat burn across my cheeks as I got his meaning.

"These are pajama bottoms," I said.

He ran a hand over my thighs, sending shivers through me as I felt his touch through the thin cotton.

"They're cute," he said. "Little bears."

I just looked at him. This man actually had me considering wearing my pajamas to Starbuck's.

"Besides," he said. "This is Birmingham. It's not like there are going to be that many people there."

I couldn't believe I was even considering this.

But the only other clothes I had brought with me were business skirts and jackets.

It was either go put on a skirt and silk blouse, my dirty jeans from yesterday, or wear these pajama pants.

I hadn't even had a shower yet. I never left the house without a shower.

Taking a deep breath, I looked into his smiling eyes.

What the hell?

76

COOPER

*O*kay. So I might have been wrong. A little bit.

Wynter looked at me skeptically as I opened her car door.

My parents had three cars. My father's pickup truck, my mother's luxury BMW, and extra sedan that they rarely drove.

We took the sedan since the keys were hanging by the door in the kitchen.

I held out a hand for Wynter to help her out of the car.

"Nobody cares," I said.

"You're right. She stood up and lifted her chin.

I felt a little guilty for telling her that it wouldn't be crowded, but I liked it that I had enough influence over her that she did this for me.

This small action gave me hope that maybe... just maybe... she cared enough about me to call me her boyfriend in truth.

I couldn't help but worry that she was still just flirting with me about that and not serious.

It had taken me next to no time for it to become real for me.

We walked inside and fortunately, no one paid either of us

any attention. Everyone in here was in a hurry to get their own order and get to work.

We were probably the only ones here this early in the morning who weren't on our way to work.

They said that when you knew. You knew.

And I knew that Wynter was the one.

I'd never really believed that it could be that simple. I'd always thought that knowing who the right girl was would take a lot of agonized thought. After all, forsaking all others was not a small ask.

But I had absolutely no interest in any others and couldn't foresee ever having any.

I just didn't know how to know if she felt the same way.

She smiled at me as we waited in line.

Whatever nervousness she'd had about wearing her cute pajama bottoms in public seemed to have faded.

When we got to the register, she ordered her latte exactly like she'd told me earlier.

"Vanilla latte. Skinny. Extra vanilla. Extra hot." She also ordered a biscuit.

When it was my turn, I said. "I'll have the same."

The smile she bestowed in my direction was worth it for me to drink a hot coffee instead of a cold brew like I'd initially been planning on ordering.

Like a couple, quite comfortable with each other, we waited, hand-in-hand for them to make our coffees and breakfast.

Other customers waited with us, all listening for their names to be called. Behind us, people mostly tapped on their phones.

"You're right," she said.

"Right about what?" I asked, bringing her hand to my lips and kissing the backs of her fingers.

"Nothing," she said, smiling at me with her eyes.

77

WYNTER

*C*ooper Abrams was incorrigible. And here on his own turf, he was even worse.

Yet no matter how much I told myself that, I still liked him. Liked him liked him.

Being around him made my heart race and thoughts scatter.

I found myself doing things that I normally wouldn't do.

Like wearing my pajamas to Starbucks.

Good God. My sister Brianna would suggest I have my head examined.

I could imagine the You Tube video she could make about that if she knew it.

My next older sister was the one we all looked to for fashion guidance.

She was engaged now and I'd never seen her happier.

I tucked in my jade green silk blouse and straightened my black pencil skirt. Brianna insisted that the green brought out the green in my eyes. All of us girls, including our mother had green eyes, so she should know.

Running the straight iron through my hair, I considered my reflection.

Halfway down one strand, I froze.

I looked just downright happy.

Not rushed or distracted or bored.

Just happy.

I quickly moved the straight iron to keep from burning the strand of hair off and leaned toward the mirror.

So this what it felt like.

Who would have thought.

Cooper was wrong for me in so many ways.

First of all, he was from Alabama and everyone knew that Texans had it going on.

Second, he was a pilot.

I was well indoctrinated into the dangers of bonding with a pilot.

They were never home.

They couldn't be trusted.

Why… Daddy had disappeared on Momma for twenty years. Then she'd taken him back.

Talk about criticism. Everyone wanted to know why Savannah would forgive Noah for leaving her like that.

But she did.

And he'd proven himself worthy of forgiveness every day of his life since then.

In fact… Momma never talked bad about pilots. I'd never heard her say anything bad about the profession.

It was my sisters who'd come up with those rules.

And being the youngest, I'd just followed their lead.

Ha. I'd never had a reason to doubt them.

Although… every single one of them had broken their own rules.

I'd been doing my own thing and hadn't really paid attention.

But now I was paying attention, wasn't I?

And I was pretty sure I'd gone and broken rule number

three.

Never fall in love with a pilot.

78

COOPER

"I can go ahead and go," Mother said.

"If you want to," I said, looking over my shoulder at my mother.

She was understandably a nervous wreck. Despite my father's ridiculous work ethic that led to him rarely being home, when he was home, he was present for her and they had a solid relationship.

Better than what he had with me. I think he had trouble understanding me because I was different. The only one of his children who hadn't gone to business school. The only one who'd left the state to do his own thing. A pilot, of all things.

And yet I was the one he called when he needed to travel. He mostly traveled to Alaska where his father had retired and moved a few years ago.

I admired everything about Grandpa. He'd been the entrepreneur. He was the one who'd started the original bank and trust. Had established the business and got it successful to leave to his only child—my father.

Once Father was firmly in place and had proven that he could keep it going, Grandpa had retired. Left it to my Father.

Grandpa would have been my perfect role model, but there was one hitch and I hadn't decided how to feel about it yet.

Grandpa just kept on working. No matter where he went, he kept working. It was like it was in his blood.

He wanted to open a branch in Alaska. I didn't know who he had in mind to run that branch, but I'm certain he had someone.

One of his grandsons and granddaughter. There were four brothers and two sisters to pull from. There would have been five brothers, but I didn't count. I'd gone a completely different way.

The clock on the mantle chimed nine times. My mother was fit to be tied. She wanted to be there when the doctor made his rounds.

I was just about to tell her to go ahead. That Wynter and I would make our way to the hospital when she came down.

Then Wynter appeared at the top of the staircase, looking flustered.

She was wearing a black skirt and jacket and white sneakers. She'd told me that she only had business clothes and she apparently wasn't lying. Somehow her dress shoes had gotten in her other suitcase—the one her father flew back to house.

It was a testament to the spontaneous decision she'd made to come with me yesterday that she was unprepared. Wynter struck me as a person who never went anywhere unprepared.

"I am so sorry," she said looking from me to my mother. "I would have told you to go ahead, but a client called and it was something of any emergency."

"It's okay," I said, holding out a hand.

Mother glanced at her watch.

"It's not your fault," she said. "I should have just gone ahead or just stayed. That's what I should have done."

Wynter looked at me as we followed my mother out to the garage.

"You can drive," she said, handing the keys to me. "I'm a nervous wreck."

Mother climbed into the passenger seat, leaving Wynter to ride in the backseat.

None of us said two words on the twenty-minute drive to the hospital.

Mother was preoccupied about being there to talk with Father's doctor. Wynter was probably feeling like it was her fault for running late.

And I was just generally in a foul mood. For some reason my whole family was being shitty toward Wynter.

I looked at her in the rearview mirror. She was biting her lip and staring out the window.

Didn't they know?

Couldn't they see?

Wynter was the girl I was going to marry.

79

WYNTER

I sat in the hospital waiting room. Alone. While Cooper was with his mother in Mr. Abram's room talking with the doctor.

He'd said I could come with them, but I politely declined.

Mrs. Abrams was already perturbed with me for making her late.

I thought it best to keep my distance for a while.

Besides, this was a personal family matter. I was a total stranger, really.

Just because his son had given me a mind-blowing orgasm that morning, all clothing intact, didn't suddenly make me part of the family.

I had no right to intrude on such a private appointment.

The way Mrs. Abrams was acting, I was kinda surprised that Cooper was even in there. But Cooper was his son and apparently he was the only one of their seven children who had made themselves available this morning.

In my family, all five of us would have been there.

But we were different.

My family was close. I'd heard people say that we were too close, but none of us paid them any attention.

That was the thing about the Worthington family. We did what we wanted and the rest of the world need not approve.

Both my mother and my father were two of the most giving people I'd ever met. And I didn't think that just because they were my parents.

At any rate, I had some emails to catch up on, so I'd pulled out my iPad, found a table to use as a desk, and went to work.

To be honest, I needed the time to catch up on work.

Cooper had been a huge distraction since the day I'd met him.

And it wasn't getting any better.

I was deep into my work, so time passed quickly. It was at least an hour later when Cooper came out to find me.

I closed the lid on my laptop.

"Everything okay?" I asked.

"Better than okay," he said. "They're sending him home."

"Today?" I asked. "Now?"

I knew that hospitals were trying to cut costs, but the man had just had surgery yesterday.

"I know." He pulled out a chair and sat down next to me. "It's really unexpected."

"So now what?" I asked.

"My older sister is on her way and I think the whole family will be over tonight."

My stomach dropped at meeting the whole Abrams clan.

"Do I need to call Daddy?" I asked. "To have him send for me?"

He sat back in his chair.

"Do you have somewhere you need to be?"

"Not for a few days," I said. "But—"

Cooper shook his head.

"Cooper," I said. "I feel like I'm intruding."

"Nope," he said, putting a hand over mine. "Stay with me."

I smiled. There was really nothing I wanted more.

But as much as I wanted to be with Cooper, I was as wary of his family.

So far, my reception had been less than warm.

80

COOPER

*G*etting my father home had turned out to be a bigger ordeal than anyone expected. He'd actually ended up going home by ambulance.

Apparently the Abrams name carried enough weight around here that Daddy had not only gone home in an ambulance, but Mother had been able to hire a nurse to stay with him once he got there.

Back at home, Mother went about the business of making everything comfortable for Father.

And since all the family was coming in tonight, she tossed a bunch of the details to me.

I didn't really mind. At least I wouldn't have minded, except that I really wanted to focus on Wynter.

Actually as a pilot, I was accustomed to taking care of details similar to this. Not to scale, but a lot of passengers had small unique requests that had to be filled. And us pilots flying private aircrafts were the ones who had to fill those requests.

Still. I wasn't used to having family things fall on my shoulders.

Wynter offered to help, but I asked her to sit with Father.

Whether or not that had been a good idea was still up for debate.

But mother was running around with a million things on her mind and I was handling the food and drinks for tonight.

Since Wynter had such a good relationship with her own father, I thought she might hit it off with mine.

And I had another motive. I wanted them to get to know each other.

I was counting on my father being nice to her.

If he wasn't, it would be three strikes and I would go back to Houston, leaving the Abrams family to fend for themselves.

I peeked into the room set up for Father on the first floor a couple of times and so far, so good.

The first time, Wynter was handing him a glass of ice while he was telling her something about Alaska.

"You've never been there?" I heard him ask her.

"Never," she said.

"You should definitely go…" Father said.

I walked off, my phone to my ear.

He was being nice to her, so all was going well.

Just as I disconnected my call, Mother stopped me in the hallway.

"Is that girl really your girlfriend?" she asked.

I took a deep breath.

The questions were starting sooner than I expected. Mother was supposed to be focused on Father and on having everyone over tonight.

"Yes," I said, owning the surge of pride.

"Do you know anything about her?" Mother asked. "Have you vetted her to make sure she's from a good family?"

I looked at my mother with total disbelief.

First of all, she should trust my judgement.

When had I ever brought a girl home who wasn't from a

good family and even if Wynter didn't meet the standards of what Mother considered a good family, I wouldn't have cared.

I lowered my voice and spoke very clearly as I answered her.

"Mother," I said. "you should be asking yourself if we're a good family for her. And from what I've seen so far by the way she's been received by all of you, I'm erring on the edge of no."

81

WYNTER

r. Abrams was such a nice man. He was so nice that he made up for the way Cooper's mother and his brother had been.

I understood that they were under a lot of stress, so I wouldn't hold it against them. Besides, the man they were so stressed over was worth all the fuss, in my opinion.

I had a feeling Cooper took after his father.

"Next time Cooper goes to Alaska to visit his grandfather," Mr. Abrams said. "get him to take you with him."

"Maybe I'll do that," I said with a grin.

The room smelled like antiseptic and looked a lot like a hospital room, too. With monitors and trays and a rolling cart.

Had someone told Mr. Abrams that Cooper and I were dating?

Dating wasn't even the right word. We hadn't been on a date.

Dating was a relative term.

Cooper and I had half-way planned our future. The important parts anyway, like pets and children and where we would live.

But for all I knew, that whole conversation had been an exercise in flirtation.

Or maybe we were doing the dating process backwards.

Either way, I was enjoying Mr. Abram's company.

"Do you think you'll ever move to Alaska?" I asked. "like your father?"

"Oh no," he said. "Actually I've never given it a thought. There's so much work to do here."

I nodded. "Probably. But it seems like you have competent children in place to run your business."

"I do," he said. "I have no doubt about that."

He looked into my eyes.

"You know which one of children has impressed me the most?" he asked.

Probably Cooper or he wouldn't be bringing it up.

"Which one?" I asked.

"Cooper," Mr. Abrams said, then looked off into space.

I smiled. "I'm listening."

"The rest of my children, bless their hearts, followed a prescribed plan. They followed a path already laid out for them. But not Cooper. Cooper blazed his own path. He followed his heart."

Mr. Abrams looked back at me.

"I hope he continues to follow his heart in his personal life as well."

"I hope so, too," I said.

He patted my hand.

"So tell me," he said. "What exactly are they planning for me tonight? Because I could never tell my wife, but I hate surprises."

I laughed. "I honestly don't know. They sent me away." I leaned closer and lowered my voice. "I think they were afraid I'd tell you."

Mr. Abrams laughed, then stopped abruptly and put a hand

up to his chest. "Don't make me laugh, Child. You can't know how much it hurts me."

"Alright," I said, wiping the smile off my face. "I won't make you laugh anymore. But smiling is okay, right?"

"Smiling is the best medicine," he said.

Then he looked up as the nurse came up to his bed. "But don't tell her. She thinks she has the best medicine."

The nurse looked at me.

"Actually, Mr. Abrams," she said. "I have to agree with you. But…" She aimed a thermometer at his forehead. "We won't tell the doctors. Deal?

"Deal," he said.

I looked over toward the door to see Cooper standing there smiling at me.

Just looking at him made my blood spin through my veins.

82

COOPER

*I*t wasn't a party. Not exactly. It was more of celebration.

Father had undergone major surgery and now he was home.

I'd finally learned exactly what kind of surgery. A heart catheterization. It could have been a whole, whole lot worse.

There was a veil of relief over the whole family.

With the help of the nurse, I got Father into the living room and into his chair. All of his adult children were here tonight. Grandpa wasn't coming. Mother had convinced him to wait a few days to come down so they could actually enjoy him being here.

There were seven of us and two spouses. No grandchildren. Not yet.

Unlike some of our other gatherings, there was no pizza. No chips and salsa.

Instead, we all had maple orange salmon and sweet potatoes with mango salsa. Close enough. And heart healthy.

And I had to say that it was quite good. There were worse ways to eat.

And there was no alcohol.

All this in respect for Father's condition.

I didn't know how long it was going to last—this eating healthy—for him or us, but it was certainly a step in the right direction.

Wynter and I sat on a little love seat by the front window, balancing our plates on our laps, our bottles of water at our feet.

"Not the way we usually eat," I said.

"I think your father is enjoying this," she said, looking over at me before she took a bite of salmon. "So it really doesn't matter, does it?"

I shook my head, feeling moisture welling in my eyes.

Two days ago, I hadn't been sure that my father would be around for a gathering like this.

I shook off the despondency and smiled at Wynter. This was not the time for feeling sad.

Father was here. He was doing great. My whole family was here.

As things began to quiet down as we finished eating, Mr. Abrams stood up.

His nurse rushed to steady him, but he really didn't need it.

"I'd like to make a toast," he said.

There was a bit of laughter as water bottles were located.

Father held up his bottle.

"To my family," he said. "For pulling together and being there. And..." he made a dramatic pause. "To Wynter Worthington. The newest member of our family."

There was silence. I just stared at my father.

Then I looked at Wynter.

"I didn't say anything to him," she whispered.

My oldest sister laughed, relieving some of the tension in the room.

"To Wynter," she held up her bottle in a toast.

Then she looked over at us. "Don't worry," she said. "Father did the same thing to Todd when we first started dating."

Father sat down and everyone went back to eating and talking about whatever they had been talking about before Father's mysterious toast.

Wynter leaned over and whispered to me.

"Are we dating?" she asked.

I grinned at her.

"Hell yes," I said. Then I winked at her. "Father has a sense about these things."

"A sense, huh?" she said, taking a bite of her baked sweet potato.

"Yep," I said. "I never really like sweet potatoes, but these aren't half bad."

"They're actually really good," Wynter said. "I've never seen them with salmon."

And just like that we slid right into a being a comfortable couple talking about sweet potatoes and salmon.

83

WYNTER

*I*t was hard not to compare the Abrams' celebratory dinner with my family's gatherings.

After the Abram's finished dinner, they hung around, talking some to Mr. Abrams. But it wasn't long before they began to scatter.

Most everyone stopped over to say how nice it was to meet me, though I could tell they really didn't quite know what to think.

"You don't bring too many girls home, do you?" I asked after about half his family had left to go to their respective homes. All seven of the Abrams children, it appeared, lived somewhere not here, but within driving distance.

Cooper looked at me funny.

"I haven't brought a girl home since high school," he said.

"Huh." I sat back, balancing my water bottle on one knee. "And you don't come home much either."

"That is very astute of you Dr. Worthington," Cooper said.

"I never told you I have a Ph.D." I looked at him sideways.

"There's a lot of information on the Internet," he said, "and I had some free time. Although..."

"Although what?" I tipped my bottle back and drank some of the cool water. I actually found it refreshing to have a healthy meal with water.

Maybe I'd do it more often. There was something to be said for tipping the scales in the direction of longevity.

"Although I have to admit that you're better hidden than most."

"Hidden how?"

"When I was researching Skye Travels for my interview, I didn't see anything about you."

"It's probably a bit strange," I said. "but I don't really do social media."

"Why is that strange?" he asked.

Mr. Abrams was saying good night to one of his sons.

I should probably have been paying more attention because I couldn't have called his name if I'd had to.

"It's strange," I said. "because my sister Brianna is all over You Tube."

"I don't think it's strange. Actually I don't think it's a bad thing to stay away from it. I think people put too much personal information out there for the world to see.

"I am private," I said. "More so than most people, I guess."

"This bothers you, then?" he asked. "This large family gathering?"

"This?" I said. "I'm used to this. I mean... I need to take some time to learn everyone's names, but this is nothing."

"My family is bigger than yours."

I shoved my hair back off my face.

"Three of my sisters have husbands or fiancés, and Daddy is always bringing people home from work. So we aren't at a loss for having people around."

Cooper reached over and took my hand.

"Can you imagine both of our families together?"

My eyes widened.

"Now that," I said. "is a little bit scary."

And, I had to admit a valid reason for an elopement.

84

COOPER

I helped the nurse get Father into bed.

When I came out of his room, Wynter had already gone upstairs.

I'd told her to. I'd just secretly hoped that she would wait up for me.

I went up to my bedroom and changed into my night clothes. Pajama bottoms and a t-shirt. Not so different from what I'd gotten Wynter to wear to Starbuck's this morning.

I winced as I brushed my teeth. I wouldn't want to wear this out in public.

I had to admit that Wynter was a good sport.

Damn. I missed her already.

I took out my phone.

Somewhere along the way, I'd gotten her phone number.

I opened a message to her. Hesitated.

What the hell.

ME: *Good night.*

I hoped she wasn't already asleep. If she was like me, she'd have her phone on Do Not Disturb.

But a message came right back.

WYNTER: *Good night.*

I held the phone. Wondering what else I could say to her.

I didn't want to say something wrong. But I didn't want to say good night yet. Not really.

ME: *Do you have everything you need?*

The little response bubbles popped up. Then vanished. Maybe she was having trouble knowing what to say, too.

I smiled to myself.

WYNTER: *Maybe not.*

I stared at my phone. Had she misunderstood my question?

ME: *What can I do?*

Little bubbles popped up. Then vanished.

I sat down on the edge of the bed and waited.

Now there was no way I was going to get any sleep.

WYNTER: *I'm sure you'll think of something.*

I laughed out loud.

She was flirting with me.

I started to type something, but stopped.

ME: *I don't even know where you are.*

WYNTER: *The guest room.*

ME: *There are four of them.*

Silence.

The minutes ticked past.

WYNTER: *Then I guess there's nothing you can do.*

ME: *There's always something I can do.*

After I hit send, I laughed at myself.

That was a rather cocky thing for me to say.

But I really did believe I could figure this thing out.

No response. Not even thought bubbles.

ME: *Easy.*

ME: *Just step outside your door.*

WYNTER: *Sounds like cheating.*

Cheating? Really? It sounded logical to me.

WYNTER: *Ok.*

I was off the bed in two seconds and had my hand on the doorknob.

But I purposely waited. Counted to ten. Then opened the door and stepped into the hallway.

It was quiet in the hallway. Quiet and cool. And dark.

Markedly different from when I'd been growing up. There had been all sorts of different music spilling out from our rooms along with conversations. Typical teenagers talking on the phone late into the night.

I stood and waited. My room was in the middle, so Wynter's guest room could be on either side of me.

I heard the door to the right of me opening. Mother had given Wynter my older sister's room.

It was probably the best room as far as guest rooms went. It actually looked like a guest room and not a storage room for things the kids had left behind. Or a hobby room where Father kept his fly-fishing ties.

She was wearing her teddy bear pajamas and, but a different t-shirt from the one she'd worn this morning. This one was a dark gray.

She saw me and smiled.

I closed the distance between us and wrapped her in my arms.

Enough with the games.

I wanted her in my arms.

Putting one hand behind her knees, I picked her up and planted a kiss on her lips.

Kissing her had become my favorite pastime. It even rivaled flying.

Hell. Who was I kidding?

If I had to pick one over the other, I'd have to pick kissing Wynter any day of the week.

She wrapped her arms around my neck and matched me kiss for kiss, our tongues sliding together in sheer intimacy.

I needed to get her out of the hallway.

Pushing open her door, I stepped inside and let her slide to her feet. Our lips never separating.

I backed up until my knees touched the bed. I sat down and pulled her into my lap.

Now this was the right way to end the day.

85

WYNTER

*C*ooper's kisses made my knees weak.

I held onto him. My arms wrapped securely around his neck. But if he let go, I'd fall to the floor. That was just how weak in the knees he left me.

He moved back, sitting more securely on the bed, taking me with him.

Something unexpected occurred to me as he kissed me senseless.

It occurred to me that I could not sleep with him.

No matter how much I wanted to. No matter how right it felt, I couldn't do it.

It would not be in my best interest.

Somewhere along the way… maybe from the beginning… I'd fallen in love with Cooper Abrams. Love at first sight?

And sleeping with him could put our relationship at risk.

My thoughts scattered in about a hundred different directions at once.

And while my thoughts were at war with one another, my lips couldn't get enough of his.

I felt like I was in a trance... under his spell... I couldn't stop kissing him.

And then after time had passed... after I was drunk off his kisses... he fell backwards and took me with him.

That movement jarred me back to reality.

"I can't," I said.

He froze.

Then he sat up on the edge of the bed and held out a hand to help me up, too.

My blood was still pumping too fast through my veins. I pressed my hands together to keep them from visibly trembling.

"What's happened?" he asked, looking at me with hooded eyes. His lips were swollen too and with his five o'clock shadow, he looked almost more handsome than I could bear to look at.

So I looked down at my own hands.

"What did I do?" he asked.

I couldn't tell him that I was painfully in love with him.

He'd think I was one of those girls who fell in love too quick —thinking there was a committed relationship when there really wasn't one.

I wasn't one of those girls. I flirted and played, but I didn't fall in love easily.

But I'd fallen for Cooper and I'd fallen hard.

Who would have thought?

I'd gone and broken all the rules in one fell swoop.

"Tell me what I did," he said.

I just shook my head, battling the tears that threatened to fall down my cheeks. My throat burned. I couldn't look at him and not cry.

I stood up and turned away.

"I have to go," I said over my shoulder as I left the room.

Only then did I realize that I'd just walked out of my own room.

I stood in the hallway, trying to figure out what to do next.

I needed to call Daddy. I needed to go home. But I didn't have my phone.

Turning around, I went back into my room, not making eye contact with Cooper at all.

"I need my phone," I said, grabbing my phone, then my handbag. Then I spotted my computer bag on the dresser and grabbed it, too.

With my essential belongings with me, I headed downstairs.

My hands shaking, I unlocked my phone.

"Daddy," I said when he answered. "Will you come get me?"

86

COOPER

*W*hat the hell?

I sat on the guest bed. Wynter's bed as long as she was the guest and stared at the open door.

I replayed the last hour or so.

I'd been high on her kisses, but I hadn't done anything more than kiss her.

She'd seemed to be enjoying herself.

Until she wasn't.

Her suitcase stood neatly at the foot of the bed.

She had to come back. She'd left her clothes. And not just her clothes, but her designer suitcase.

I had two sisters. I knew that a girl wouldn't leave those things behind.

Besides, she was wearing her pajamas. Normally I would have thought that she wouldn't go anywhere in her pajamas, but I'd shown her this morning that no one cared.

I should never have done that. It was backfiring on me in spades.

What I couldn't figure out was what I'd done wrong. What had I done to send her racing away from me?

She'd been receptive to everything we'd done. The kissing…
and even the other. In fact, she'd seemed to be very receptive to
grinding against me. It had seemed to even bring a smile to her
lips.

From my perspective, she'd liked it quite a bit.

I just needed to give her some space to work out whatever
it was that was going on with her.

Hell. It could be anything.

Still dazed from her kisses and confused by what had
happened, I walked down the hall to my room.

The grandfather clock downstairs began to chime the hour,
each chime echoing through the house.

I stood frozen, my hand on my doorknob, listening.
Counting.

Twelve chimes.

Midnight.

As the echoes of the chimes hung in the air, slowly fading, I
heard the front door slam.

I went to the window at the end of the hall and watched
Wynter walk down the sidewalk to the circle drive.

She had actually gone outside. What was she…

Then a car, its headlights bright, turned into the circle drive
and stopped.

It was a yellow taxi. Wynter had called a taxi.

She didn't wait for the driver to get out. She just jumped
into the back seat.

Then the taxi slowly made its way around the circle drive
back to the road.

I watched as the lights faded down the street. Until it
turned the corner.

She'd left. Just like that. She'd taken her purse and her
computer bag. But she'd left her clothes and her luggage.

She'd dashed out of the house at the stroke of Midnight and
disappeared into the night.

Just when I couldn't get enough of her.
I turned and leaned against the window casing.
No sense. It made no sense whatsoever.
There was only one explanation.
Wynter Worthington was my Cinderella.

87

WYNTER

I sat inside the airport's private terminal and waited for my father.

Most girls called their fathers in the middle of the night to drive across town to pick them up, but not me. I called my father to fly completely across two other states to pick me up.

And I didn't even have a good reason.

All I knew was that I'd panicked. I'd panicked and I'd needed to get away.

I'd have to sort it out later. Later with some distance in space and time.

I watched as the plane landed. Daddy had flown one of his smaller two-seaters. I was pretty sure he rarely used this particular plane anymore.

It had taken him less than two hours to get here from Houston. I don't know how he did it, but he always managed to be there when we needed him.

I stepped outside into the evening air and breathed in the comforting scent of jet fuel. My tears had dried, but my heart was heavy.

Daddy brought the plane to a stop and stepped out onto the tarmac.

"Where's your luggage?" he asked.

"I left it," I said.

A shadow crossed Daddy's features.

I'd only seen that look one other time. And it hadn't had anything to do with me.

"What happened?" he asked.

"Nothing," I said. "I just wanted to go home."

Daddy helped me into the plane, his expression skeptical now.

With me buckled in, he went around and settled into the pilot's seat. Flipped a couple of switches.

He looked over at me.

"Do I need to go kick somebody's ass?" he asked.

"No," I said quickly. "Please don't."

"I just..." I looked away. I didn't know how to explain it to him.

How could I explain nothing that made no sense?

I leaned my head back against the seat and closed my eyes.

But Daddy wasn't moving. He was waiting.

"Wynter," he said. "You called me in the middle of the night and asked me fly across the country to get you. The least you can do is to give me an explanation."

He was right. Oh. God. He was so right.

"Daddy," I said, turning to face him. A tear traced its way down my cheek.

He gently wiped it away.

My chin trembled. It seemed like so much was changing. My sisters all getting married. My oldest sister living in Denver. Daddy being treated for prostate cancer.

Maybe being with Mr. Abrams and seeing his family doing a similar thing to what my family had gone through with Daddy had brought it all back.

Daddy waited patiently while I tried to analyze myself. A trick that never worked. Any psychologist could tell you that.

"I got scared," I said.

"Someone hurt you," Daddy said flatly.

"No," I said quickly shaking my head. "It's not that. Not that at all."

Damn it. I'd made a mess of things. I should have just stayed put. Made my way back to Houston in the morning like a normal person would.

But no. I'd called my Daddy. And now he was ready to tear somebody apart.

I had to fix this.

"Daddy," I said. "I was getting too... attached to Cooper. I got scared. And I called you. It was stupid."

"No," Daddy said with a little smile. "You did exactly right."

He reached out and affectionately lifted a strand of my hair then let it fall. An affectionate gesture from a father to a daughter.

"Thank you," he said. "You're the only one in the family who doesn't treat me with kid gloves."

I looked at my father. Really looked at him.

Sixty years old, he was still a handsome man. Handsome and virile. He might even be in his prime.

He'd come through the bout with prostate cancer good as new. But obviously, since he hadn't tried to hide it from anyone, he was experiencing some lingering negative perceptions.

It wasn't surprising. In fact, it was to be expected. But I hadn't given it a thought.

Even I, his youngest daughter, had fallen into the trap of keeping things from him that might upset him.

But that wasn't right. Not for us. Not for him.

He was still our daddy.

And he wanted to be part of our lives.

Daddy started flipping switches. Spoke into the microphone. Getting ready for takeoff.

"I'll tell you everything," I said. "I promise."

I'd tell him. Maybe telling him would help me sort it all out in my head.

Daddy smiled over at me.

"I know you will, Kitten," he said. "After all, you got me out of my warm bed."

"It's a good thing you like flying," I said.

"Just don't tell your mother," he said with a wink.

I settled back in my seat and prepared for the flight home.

There was no need to be nervous.

I was flying with the best.

88

COOPER

Two Days Later

$\mathcal{T}$here was no reason for me to stay around Birmingham now that my father was home and recovering nicely.

So I flew back to Houston.

And I flew commercial. Something I hadn't done since I got my pilot's license.

But since I didn't know what was going on with Wynter, I didn't feel like calling Noah to send a plane for me.

It was awkward at best, since Noah himself had flown me over here. And I owed him one for it.

But I hadn't spoken with his daughter since she'd dashed out on me at Midnight.

The guy sitting in front of me leaned his chair back, pressing the chair against my knees.

Flying commercial hadn't gotten one bit better since the last time I'd flown.

"Seat up," the flight attendant said as she breezed past, not even waiting for a reply.

Fortunately the guy complied, getting out of my space.

The short flight to Houston would have felt way longer than necessary with the seat on my knees.

Yep. This had been a bad idea.

I should have manned up and called Noah.

I didn't have any luggage of my own, but Wynter's suitcase was in the overhead compartment.

I took my stewardship of her suitcase seriously. I hadn't quite figured out what I was going to do with it when I got it to Houston.

Probably just drop it off on her doorstep.

I was giving her some time and some space. And hopefully she would come to me after she'd sorted out whatever was going on with her.

It was the most I could hope for.

My phone chimed with a text message.

I glanced over my shoulder to make sure there weren't any flight attendants watched and pulled my phone out of my coat pocket.

My package was delivered.

I muted the phone and put it back in my pocket.

Well. It had seemed like a good idea when I'd ordered it. That was the day I'd been getting everything ready for Father's coming home party.

Maybe I'd gotten a little carried away.

But I'd gone with my gut.

At the end of the day, it was all a man could do when he found the perfect girl.

It was a variation of something my grandmother used to say.

If she doesn't come back it wasn't meant to be.

I scrubbed a hand over my face. I hadn't even bothered to shave in three days.

I'd shave before I went back to work. Right now I just needed to get back to Houston and get settled back in. I needed to get back into some kind routine again.

Wynter still had me reeling. Trying to figure out what had happened.

The ball was in my court.

I wasn't giving up.

I was just giving her a minute to find her way back to me.

89

WYNTER

*M*y sister was having a baby. Right now. Today.

I sat in the waiting room at the Denver hospital with my sister Brianna, Daddy, and our brother Quinn.

Momma and my older sister, Ainsley, were in the room and Madison's husband, Kade, of course.

It was a full house.

It seemed like I'd spent far too much time in hospital waiting rooms this week. First in Birmingham and now in Denver.

I'd barely gotten home when we'd gotten the call to come to Denver. Everyone scrambled to cancel their appointments. Even Momma.

A lot of flights got rescheduled, too, or pilots switched out. In a family-owned company like Skye Travels, something like the first grandchild/niece/nephew had a broad spectrum effect.

We'd met at the airport, piled into the airplane like most people piled into the family car, and flew to Denver. Daddy had flown.

I'd barely been home for two days. At least I'd gotten my laundry done and caught up on some paperwork.

The waiting room was remarkably similar to the others I'd spent time in. Both in Birmingham and Houston.

The television was on, a local channel, but was muted.

Quinn's attention was on his phone. Daddy was up. He'd walk from one side of the room where the windows where, stand there a minute, then walk to the door and look out into the hallway. Then back again.

He was pacing, but he didn't want anyone to know it. probably didn't even realize he was doing it.

Madison was his oldest child with Momma. He had another daughter, Danielle, with his first wife.

He'd been there anytime Danielle needed him over the years. She was married with children of her own.

But Daddy had room in his heart for all of us.

I was confident that if I was the one back there having a baby, he'd be doing the same thing.

Brianna sat next to me. As always, she looked like she'd just stepped out of a fashion magazine.

Yet, oddly enough, she had fewer clothes than any one of the rest of us.

It was something she worked at. She even had a very popular You Tube channel where she talked about minimalism and capsule wardrobes and anything else that she caught her attention.

I tuned in every week to watch her videos, but minimalism took far more time and energy than I had to give it.

"How was Alabama?" Brianna asked.

That was the problem with having a close family. It was almost impossible to keep everyone from knowing everything.

"It was okay," I said. She knew I went to Alabama with Cooper. Everybody knew that.

But Daddy was the only who knew the details about

Cooper. That was one thing about Daddy. He could keep a secret. He wouldn't even tell Momma unless I said it was okay.

"Madison told me you and Cooper had a thing." Brianna said.

Of course, she did. Madison had no such need to keep that to herself.

I'd had time to give what had happened with Cooper a lot of thought, but I still hadn't figured it out.

I was just going to keep my head down and let things settle where they would.

I sighed and stretched my hands out in front of me.

"I don't know what we had. I do know that a lot of rules were broken."

"Rules?" Brianna asked. "What rules?"

"You know," I said. "The rules about pilots."

Quinn looked up from his phone, but didn't say anything.

"Wynter," Brianna said. "You know that Skye Travels doesn't have any rules about not dating. If they did, we'd all still be single."

Quinn turned his attention back to his phone and Daddy walked from the window back to the door.

I didn't say anything. I was feeling a bit light-headed.

Brianna turned and looked right at me.

"What rules?" she asked. "Tell me one."

"Never crush on a pilot," I said.

Brianna stared blankly at me for a moment, then she pressed her fingertips against her forehead.

"Wynter," she said. "You don't think those are real rules, do you?"

"But you and Ainsley…"

Brianna held up her left hand with a big diamond sitting on her ring finger.

"If those were real rules, do you think I'd be getting

married… to a pilot." She swept a hand around the room. "Everybody in this family is either a pilot or married to a pilot."

"Except Quinn," I said, grasping at the first thing that came to mind.

"Quinn doesn't count," she said.

"Why not?"

My brother was something of a mystery to me. He was quiet and serious, but he was always busy.

The only boy in a family with four sisters couldn't possibly have been easy for him.

"Because he does his own thing," she said. "So you had a crush on Cooper. What's the next rule?"

"Never kiss a pilot."

Brianna looked at me with mock seriousness.

"You did *not* kiss him?" she asked.

I couldn't help but smile.

"I did kiss him," I said, remembering just how much I'd kissed him and just how wonderful it had been.

"If Madison ever gets this baby born, we've got some things to talk about."

90

COOPER

*W*heels down. Adjust for drag. Prepare for landing.

Flying into Denver was different from flying into Houston. The mountain air changed things.

I'd made a quick turnaround, leaving the next morning right after I got back into Houston.

The snow-capped Rocky Mountains never failed to pull at my heart. Majestic and beautiful.

As a youth, I'd spent some time up in the mountains with my grandparents on my mother's side. They'd always planned on retiring and moving up here to the live in the mountains but they'd both died early.

I tried to remember the good times I'd had with them in the mountains, but days like today I couldn't help but think about the lost hopes and dreams. Plans that never came to fruition.

I didn't want my life to be like that. Everywhere I turned, I kept seeing reminders not to live for tomorrow.

My father. My grandparents.

Grandpa, living in Alaska, was the closet role model I had for someone fully living their dreams.

Grandpa had done it right. He'd made his money early enough that he could enjoy life in Alaska. But he was fortunate, too. Fortunate to be in good enough health to enjoy the way of life he'd earned.

I went in for a landing, my wheels touching smoothly on the runway.

I'd gotten a text from Noah, asking me to bring a plane to Denver.

Apparently Madison was having her baby and although the whole family had flown up to Denver together, they were wanting to leave at different times.

I didn't know who I was picking up.

But no matter who it was, my stomach was torn up with nervousness at seeing Wynter.

I wanted to see her, but I was worried, too.

Worried that she wouldn't want to see me.

I'd known better than to play where I worked.

But I'd gone and done it anyway. Now I had to deal with the consequences.

I wasn't giving up. I was just backing off.

After she had time to get over whatever it was that had sent her running, I was going to start over again.

Go at it straight this time. From the beginning.

Drinks. Dinner.

I taxied over to the terminal.

I didn't know who I was fooling.

Wynter and I could never go back to the basics. We'd come too far.

We knew too much about each other.

I didn't even want to go back to the basics with her.

I patted my jacket pocket. I knew exactly what I wanted. And I wasn't going to give up without a fight.

I'd fight a whole war if I had to.

91

WYNTER

*M*adison and baby went home the next day.
Sophia Skye Johnson.
Seven pounds and three ounces.

They had no reason for naming her Sophia other than liking it, but Skye was in honor of Momma's middle name. Besides, it just seemed fitting to name her Skye.

I was an aunt now. Aunt Wynter.

It was kind of exciting, but none of us knew anything about babies. We'd never babysat like most girls did as teens because, well… we didn't need the money.

And we'd been encouraged to focus on school and hobbies instead.

It had served us all well, except that now Momma was the only one of us who knew anything about babies.

But we were learning and learning fast.

They say it takes a village. And we had a village ready and willing.

Madison was in bed, sitting up against a mound of pillows, watching us with a little smile. She looked exhausted. exhausted and happy all rolled into one.

My sister Ainsley, a pilot, was the most tomboyish one of us girls. She was the last one I would have expected to get all mushy about a baby.

"Look at her little fingers," Ainsley said. "and toes. They're so perfect."

"Of course they are," Kade said. He was trying to be cool, but it was obvious he was a proud father. And right now he was hovering over Sophia, keeping watch over her even with all of us in the room.

"Can I hold her?" Ainsley asked, looking up at Kade with puppy-dog eyes.

We all looked at Madison and Kade. They hadn't let anyone except Momma hold her so far.

Kade reached down and picked Sophia up like she was made of fragile glass and carefully set her in Ainsley's arms.

"Make sure to hold her head up," he said.

"I know," Ainsley said. Then she was cooing and talking nonsense to Sophia.

"Never expected that," I said to no one in particular.

Momma just smiled.

"You just never know," she said.

"We should go shopping," Brianna said. "Buy her some designer clothes. Some shoes."

"We will," Madison said. "Let her get used to breathing air before you start dressing her up."

"It's never too early," Brianna said.

I watched my sisters interacting with each other and Sophia.

Brianna held her next, with Ainsley finally giving her up, not without reluctance.

I had the distinct sense that our lives would never be the same again.

Again, that sense that everything was changing swept over

me like a veil. In a good way. Change was good, right? But the change was leaving me unsettled.

I never really thought this day would come. This day when us girls were all grown up, getting married and having babies.

But it was here.

"Your turn, Wynter," Brianna said, bringing Sophia over to me.

"I don't think so," I said, with a glance at Kade. But Kade was sitting on the bed with Madison, apparently having gotten over some of his initial wariness. Or maybe he'd just given up. It was hard for anyone to win against the Worthington girls, especially when we were all together.

"You have to," Brianna said. "she's your niece."

"I know," I said, "but I don't know how."

"Seriously?" Ainsley asked. "Is that what you're going with? Because this is the first time I've ever held a baby."

"I've held a baby before," Brianna said.

All three of us looked at her.

"Who?" Ainsley asked in an accusatory tone as though Brianna had somehow cheated on us.

"Danielle's baby," she said. "Remember? Our half-sister has had four babies."

"Right," Ainsley said, dismissing the whole conversation. "You might as well leave her alone."

"Why?" Brianna asked. "Why wouldn't she want to—?" Brianna stopped. Looked at me. Then held Sophia in my direction. "Time to come out of your funk," she whispered for my ears only.

She was giving me no choice. No choice but to take Sophia. I shot her a withering glance, but gathered Sophia into my arms.

My heart tripped up on itself. She was so little. So small and perfect. And beautiful.

I turned my back to everyone, my heart swelling with such unexpected emotion.

This tiny newborn baby was one of us. She was a Worthington.

The world was brand new for her and she could do anything. It was up to us to introduce her to life.

She looked at me with curious, happy eyes. I didn't care if others said she was too young. I stood by what I saw.

"Welcome to the world," I said, softly, to just her.

Somewhere in the back of my mind, I heard Daddy come into the room.

"Where's Wynter?" he asked. "There's someone here to see her."

I was so overcome with emotion I didn't care about seeing anybody.

"Wynter," Daddy said and I turned automatically.

But Daddy wasn't who I saw when I turned.

Cooper stood just inside the bedroom door next to Daddy.

Our gazes met and held.

I needed to sit down.

92

COOPER

*W*hether or not it was true didn't matter. I'd go to my grave believing that Noah had not only summoned me to Denver under the guise of needing an airplane, but he'd tricked me into coming here to Madison's apartment where Wynter was.

A driver had been waiting for me at the airport—very unusual in itself for a driver to be waiting for a pilot. Noah had met me at the door to Madison's apartment. He'd stood there a moment, looking at me as though he was trying to figure something out.

Then he said. "You're here. That's a start."

"Sir?"

But instead of answering me, he turned and waved me to follow him upstairs.

I heard women talking. Was I supposed to be up here.

I stopped at the door.

"What's going on?" I asked.

"A happy occasion," Noah said. "You need to be here."

At first I didn't see Wynter. Just her sisters.

Then when Noah called out to her a second time, she turned.

The rest of the world faded away and I nearly came undone.

Wynter stood there, cradling an infant in her arms.

And it wasn't so much that she was holding the infant as it was the way she looked. Her expression was so soft and full of love and vulnerable that my own breath caught.

"Wynter," I breathed then without thinking I closed the distance between us.

Careful of the baby between us, I put my arms around her and kissed her forehead.

Then I shifted back and looked down at the baby.

"Madison's?" I asked, knowing full well who she was.

"Yes," Wynter said, her voice husky. "Her name is Sophia Skye."

"It's a perfect name for her," I said, lightly touching a hand against the baby's cheek.

Wynter searched my eyes.

"Why are you here?" she asked. "Why?"

"Divine intervention, I guess."

Kade stepped up next to us.

"Sophia's mother is asking for her," he said, carefully taking Sophia out of Wynter's arms.

Wynter gave her up, with what looked like more than a bit of reluctance.

She watched Kade and the baby for a moment, then turned back to me. She blinked, then focused on me.

"So how are you here?" she asked again.

I glanced over my shoulder.

"Something to do with your father," I said.

She looked over my shoulder for Noah, but he'd already pulled up a chair next to Madison and wasn't paying us any attention.

"That figures," she said, looking back into my eyes. "I guess we need to talk."

It didn't matter who said those words or in what context. They struck fear all the way to the core.

I didn't say anything. I didn't have to. I just followed her out of the bedroom to the living room downstairs.

93

WYNTER

I sat on the sofa in Madison's living room and Cooper sat next to me.

As always when he was around, my hands were trembling, so I clasped them together.

I reminded myself that he was here because Daddy had summoned him here. Not because he wanted to be here.

I looked over at him from beneath my lashes and took a deep breath. I needed to just get this over with.

Rip off the band-aid quick.

"I'm sorry," I said.

He nodded. "I wish I knew what I did. So I won't do it again."

His words gave me hope and the courage to go on. He was speaking in the future tense. Like there was hope that I would have another chance.

"You didn't do anything wrong," I said.

"I must have done something," he said. "for you to dash off like Cinderella."

"Cinderella?"

"You even left a slipper behind."

I looked straight at him now. "I don't wear slippers."

"Might as well be a slipper," he said. "You left your suitcase."

"I guess I did," I said. My heart was feeling a bit lighter. He didn't seem mad. Just confused.

I was confused, too, and I was the one who'd done it.

"What did you tell your father?" he asked.

"Everything," I said, trying not to wince.

"It's a wonder he didn't punch me in the face."

"I don't think he'd do that," I said, but the expression he'd made was burned into my brain and I honestly wasn't so very sure that he wouldn't have done just that if he'd thought I'd been wronged.

"So..." he said. "maybe you could tell me at least part of what's going on. So I can understand."

"I just needed to..." How much was I supposed to tell him? This wasn't one of those flirt with 'em and leave 'em kind of relationships. This was more.

At least I hoped it was more. To me it was more.

And that was where the problem started.

"I was feeling like I..." I said, then stopped again.

Just say it. spit it out.

How many times had I told people to do just that?

Like it was the easiest thing in the world to do.

"I was starting to believe in the things we were saying," I said.

"Like what?" he asked.

I lowered my gaze. Took a deep breath, but before I could form an answer, someone was coming down the stairs.

"Let's take a walk," he said, standing up and holding out a hand.

I put my hand in his.

"Okay."

We slipped out the front door and walked to the sidewalk leading back to a little park.

"I didn't even know this was here," I said.

The spruce and fir trees filled the air with what smelled like Christmas in May. The scent was in contrast to the little white daisies reaching toward the warm springtime sunshine. As we sat on a little wooden bench, butterflies drifted from one flower to another.

"I knew," he said. "I knew it was here."

"How did you know?" I asked.

"I was here before, remember?"

"I remember."

And that was part of the problem. I couldn't get him out of my head.

I kept remembering his kisses.

He was clean-shaven now. He must have flown up from Houston today. Pilots had to be clean-shaven to fly.

I couldn't get him out of my head. I'd thought that maybe some distance would help, but it hadn't.

It had only made my heart long for him more. And now that he was here, I couldn't even talk to him.

What kind of mixed-up-ness was that?

"I started to think that our relationship was real." I said. "And that we were doing more than just playing around." I took a deep breath. "So I had to get away to straighten out my head."

The problem was that I hadn't straightened out anything.

94

COOPER

*a*t first I thought I'd heard her wrong.

Wynter didn't know if we were real or not.

A little blue butterfly landed on a white daisy near my foot.

I breathed in deeply, letting the fresh scent of the fir trees calm my senses.

But she looked genuinely troubled. She was seriously struggling with this.

"Wynter," I said, sliding close and wrapping an arm around her.

I pulled her close with my other hand until her head was tucked against my chest.

I ran my fingers through her soft hair until I felt her relax against me.

"I'm sorry," she said. "I overreacted."

"I don't think you overreacted. Panicked maybe."

"Yeah," she laughed softly. "I panicked."

"You didn't have to do that," I said.

A gust of wind tossed some leaves around and sent the butterflies away.

"I think I just got carried away in the moment," she said.

"That's not always a bad thing," I said. "I got carried away, too."

She didn't say anything.

"Wynter?" I nudged her head up so I could look into her beautiful green eyes.

"It's real," I said. "And it isn't just you."

She sat up straight and peered into my eyes, searching. Probably trying to see if I was sincere.

"How do I know?" she asked softly.

I looked straight ahead, past the little apartment complex to the Rocky Mountains towering overhead. Their snow-capped peaks surrounded by clouds. It was snowing up there.

I'd like to drive up into the mountains with Wynter and see if for myself. Go by Estes Park where I used to hang out with my grandparents. See what it looked like now. Through my grownup eyes. And see it through Wynter's eyes.

I wanted to see everything through her eyes.

She was my life now.

And I wanted to have babies with her. To see her looking down with love at our child the way she'd looked down at Madison's.

All I had to do was to find a way to tell her these things.

I wanted to tell her these things without frightening her away again.

I laced my fingers with hers.

"How do you know anything?" I asked.

When she didn't answer, I realized she didn't know what I was really asking.

"Seriously," I said. "How do you know?"

"I just have to believe," she said.

I nodded slowly and looked back down into her eyes.

"Do you believe in us?"

Her breath hitched.

"I want to," she whispered.

I brought my hand to her lips and kissed her palm.

"If you believe it, is it true?" I asked.

"Not necessarily," she said.

"I think maybe you're thinking too much."

She smiled. "Sometimes."

95

WYNTER

I could feel Cooper's heart beating beneath the palm of my hand.

He was real. So very real.

I could feel his breath against my cheek. His hand linked with mine. His arms around me, holding me close.

This was where I wanted to be. With him. Anywhere with him.

But he was asking me if I believed in us.

"How do I know if I'm right?" I asked. "How do I know if you feel the same way?"

There. I'd said it.

Straight out loud for him to hear. Now he knew my deepest, darkest insecurity.

"Say you believe," he said.

"Why?"

"Just do it," he said, removing his arms from around me. "Close your eyes," he said.

I closed my eyes.

How was I supposed to believe when he was pulling away?

"Trust me," he said.

I did trust him, so I kept my eyes closed and said it.

"I believe." The words caught in my throat. There was too much at stake if I was wrong.

A bird chirped in the tree behind me, reminding me that despite that cool air replete with the heady scent of fir trees, it was spring in Colorado.

"Open your eyes," Cooper said.

Cooper was kneeling in front of me. Grinning.

One hand was behind his back.

"I believe, too," he said.

Then he brought a little blue box from behind his back and held it out toward me in his palm.

I immediately recognized the box. It was a Tiffany's box.

I gasped and looked into his eyes.

"I believe in us," he said.

I couldn't tear my eyes away from his.

He took the lid off the box and, setting the box on the bench, opened the box inside it.

I held my breath as he lifted the lid.

He was presenting me with a perfect round platinum diamond ring.

It was iconic and beautiful.

It was perfect.

"Wynter," he said, carefully removing the ring from the box. "Will you—?"

"Yes," I breathed, holding out my hand.

He slid the ring on my finger and then I was in his arms.

"So yes?" he asked. "You'll marry me?"

"Yes," I said. "It seemed to be the only thing I could say.

"I want you to make me a promise," he said.

"Okay," I said, holding up my finger and looking at my ring.

"Don't ever run off in the middle of the night again."

My eyes full of unshed tears of happiness I looked at him.

"I promise," I said. "Next time I run off in the middle of the night, I'll take you with me."

He laughed and pulled me close.

"Okay," he said. "I don't ever want to be apart from you again."

"What about when we have to travel?" I asked.

"Those things have a tendency to work themselves out, my love."

I knew he was right.

I also knew that life wasn't made to be lived by following rules.

Especially rules that had no purpose.

Rules that kept me away from someone I was in love with.

96

COOPER

*W*ynter and I went back inside Madison's apartment.

Her whole family was gathered in the living room.

Noah and Savannah. Ainsley and her husband Wyatt. Brianna. Even Quinn.

The only ones missing were Madison, Kade, and the baby.

When we walked through the door, everyone looked up at us.

"There they are," someone said.

There were open pizza boxes on the table.

"I told you they'd be right back," Ainsley said.

"Come on," Brianna said. "Get some pizza."

This was so much like my family... only they looked happier.

Or maybe it was just me.

I was just about walking on clouds right now.

Noah stood up, kissed his wife on the top of her head.

"Cooper. Wynter," Noah said. "Do you two have something to tell us?"

There were about what felt like a hundred eyes focused on

us right now.

"Do we?" I asked, looking down at Wynter.

She grinned up at me.

"I guess now is just about as good as any," she said. "They're all here."

"Okay," I said. "I'll follow your lead."

Wynter turned back toward her family and held up her left hand for everyone to see.

Her two sisters rushed forward and hugged her.

Wyatt came over and shook my hand. Then Noah.

It all happened in a whirlwind.

Then Savannah was there.

She pulled Wynter into a hug.

"All my daughters," she said. "are married or engaged now. I'm so proud of you Wynter. Of all of you.

Savannah looked over at me.

"It's your job to take care of her now," she said.

"Yes ma'am," I said, not sure what else to say.

"It's a big job," Savannah said, smiling.

"I know," I said, seriously.

And everyone laughed.

I looked into Wynter's smiling eyes and knew that I was the luckiest man alive.

I was engaged to the girl of my dreams and not only did I love her, I knew it was no time at all before I loved her family, too.

"Are you okay?" she asked as we settled side by side on the sofa.

"I'm better than fine," I said. "Aren't you glad you broke all the rules?"

Wynter gasped. "How did you know about the rules?"

"You're not the only girl who ever broke the rules," I said.

Wynter smiled up at me.

Then I kissed her and everything was right with the world.

97

WYNTER

Two Months Later

*T*he Anchorage airport was coming up ahead and below us. But Heaven help me, it looked like we were about to land in the water.

I looked over at Cooper. He just grinned at me.

I couldn't see his eyes because he was wearing dark sunshades. But I didn't mind. I was wearing them, too. The same ones I'd taken from him the day we'd met.

Tall buildings and even taller snow-capped mountains were on our right. From up here it looked urban and rural all at once.

It was absolutely stunning.

Cooper smoothly landed the small jet and we taxied toward the tarmac.

"What do you think?" Cooper asked.

"I wonder why I've never been here before."

"Because you had to wait until you met me," he said.

"I think you're probably right," I said, leaning over and kissing him on the cheek. "But I'm still nervous about meeting your grandfather."

Cooper began securing the plane.

"You have nothing to worry about," he said. "Grandpa's easy. You've already met the hard ones."

I laughed.

"You can say that again."

Cooper unhooked his harness and looked over at me.

"That's the real reason you left, isn't it?" he asked. "It wasn't me at all."

"Oh," I said, "it was most definitely you."

"Water under the bridge." Cooper laughed.

"Something like that."

I regretted leaving him that night, but I didn't regret the way everything had turned out.

There was a limo sitting outside the tarmac with a formally dressed driver standing outside.

"Is that for us?" I asked, not seeing anyone else around that it could be for.

"It is," he said.

I lifted my shades and looked over at the driver.

"That looks like Jeff," I said.

Cooper reached over and unhooked my harness.

"It is Jeff," he said.

"What's he doing here?"

"Looks like he's picking us up."

I sent him a sideways look, but he just laughed.

"I guess your father had something to do with it," he said.

"I'll come around," he said, "get your door."

I gathered up my handbag and checked my phone. Odd. I had a good signal. But no messages. Not a single one. It was the first time I'd ever landed anywhere and didn't have at least one message.

I felt like I'd landed in the Twilight Zone. No messages. And our driver from Houston was here. In Anchorage, Alaska.

But then Cooper opened the door and wrapped me in his arms once my feet were on the ground.

"Welcome to Alaska," he said, putting his lips on mine and kissing away all my thoughts and worries.

It didn't matter where I was, as long as I was with Cooper, I was home.

It had always been like that and it always would be.

EPILOGUE
WYNTER

With Jeff driving, I sat in the back of the limo with Cooper.

We'd skirted the city and were on a dirt road now traveling through a forest of spruce trees.

Cooper sat with one arm draped around me and held my hands tightly in his.

He seemed more excited than I'd seen him in the just over two months that I'd known him.

My heart had known he was the one I wanted to marry from the first day I'd met him. It had just taken my head a little time to catch up.

It was funny, since we'd gotten engaged, we hadn't talked anymore about anything serious like what kind of wedding we wanted, or where we were going to live, or how many children we were going to have.

It was almost like we'd moved backwards. Serious stuff first. Then we just started enjoying each other's company.

I guess it wasn't much different from being with a guy off the Internet based on a questionnaire.

But it certainly felt different.

We hadn't done any questionnaires. We'd met, gotten to know each other, and fallen in love the old-fashioned way.

I caught a glimpse of a house through the trees.

But it wasn't just a house.

"Your grandfather lives in a castle?" I asked.

"Kinda," he said.

"And you didn't think to tell me," I said.

"I wanted it to be a surprise."

We turned down the driveway and I saw a eight-car garage up ahead. Eight cars? Who needed eight cars? Especially up here.

"He has different cars for different seasons," Cooper said. "And different occasions."

I didn't say anything.

Jeff drove around to the front of the house and parked the car at the front of a circle drive.

A dog came running out to greet us.

"That looks like Ainsley's dog," I said, leaning forward. "Beau."

"I guess she brought her dog," Cooper said.

I sat back against the seat.

Maybe I'd fallen down a rabbit hole.

This was like some kind of alternate reality. I was in Alaska… yet it was like everybody was here.

Cooper got out and came around to open my door while Jeff went to retrieve the luggage.

I stood up and looked around. Cooper's grandfather did indeed live in a castle. In Alaska.

As Beau came up to me, wagging his tail, I patted him on the head and checked the tag on his collar.

"It is Beau." I turned and faced Cooper.

"You *guess* Ainsley brought her dog?"

"Grandpa doesn't mind." Cooper moved toward the door.

"Cooper," I said.

"There's Ainsley now," Cooper said.

Beau ran toward my sister and her husband as they walked toward us.

"Cooper," I said. "Why is my sister here? Is this some sort of...?" I couldn't even think about what it might be.

A meeting? Maybe Wyatt and Cooper's Grandpa were doing some business together.

Yes. That had to be it.

But then I saw Madison holding her baby.

Oh. No. Something was going on.

"Want to go inside?" Cooper asked.

"I think I need an explanation first," I said.

Cooper faced me and linked his hands with mine.

I worked to focus on him and not to look toward my sisters. I needed to figure out why they were here.

"Remember when we talked about what kind of wedding we wanted?"

"What? Yes. You said an elopement."

"And you said you wanted a big wedding."

"We were just talking."

"Now you tell me," he said with mock frustration.

"Cooper?" I asked, glancing over at where Madison and Ainsley stood talking. "What is this?"

Cooper slid his sunshades up onto the top of his head.

"This is me making you happy," he said. "I hope."

I shook my head. My thoughts were scattered and I couldn't put them together to make any sense.

"Wynter," he said, taking my hands and looking into my eyes. "Everyone is here. Both our families."

"I don't understand why." I was getting the idea, but I still didn't believe it.

"So we can get married," he said. "I don't want to wait any longer."

When I just looked blankly at him, he looked worried… uncertain.

"Are you okay with that?"

"We're getting married? Today?"

"Well, tomorrow, since—"

I threw my arms around him and he twirled me around, my feet leaving the ground.

Back on my feet, I caught my breath.

"So…" I said. "Everyone's here?"

"Look," he said, nodding toward roof of the house over the garage. This whole side of the house rooftop was a terrace.

There were over two dozen people up there behind the railing, watching us.

My parents. My sisters. Quinn.

His parents. His sisters and brothers.

All their spouses and fiancés.

Grandparents.

"Oh. My…" I said, putting a hand over my mouth. "You did this?"

"Let's just say I had a lot of help."

I turned and looked in his deep blue eyes.

"There's nothing I wouldn't do for you," he said. "I love you with all my heart."

"I love you, too."

My cheeks were damp with tears, but I didn't care.

This was the man I loved.

And from here on out, the two of us would make our own rules.

Together.

Keep reading for a preview of
Second Chance Destiny…

SECOND CHANCE DESTINY PREVIEW
NOELLE WINSTON

"*P*repare for landing."

The pilot's abrupt command was followed by the flight attendants making one last run through the aisle before taking their seats near the cockpit and buckling in.

Houston's George Bush Intercontinental Airport. Both my mother and father still called it Houston Intercontinental Airport. Though the airport was renamed when I was a child, I had no memory of it being called anything other than George Bush Intercontinental Airport.

The plane's speed slowed to stabilize the approach and the airplane continued its three-degree angle as it approached the runway. The flaps extended and the spoilers were activated to increase drag.

Ten years.

Ten years since I had been home.

In some ways, I hardly even felt like the same person.

In other ways, it felt like I'd only left yesterday and everything I'd done and experienced in between faded away into a distant memory. Nothing more than a dream.

The pitch of the plane's motor increased as the pilot made

adjustments. Either it was windy or the pilot was inexperienced.

It was a cool, crisp October day. Friday afternoon.

We made the final descent, gliding over clusters of homes in subdivisions. We were flying low enough to see the outline of swimming pools in the backyards.

As we flew over the interstate, I leaned back against the seat and checked my seatbelt. It seemed worthless compared to the five-point harness I was used to.

I pulled out my air pods and slipped them into my ears.

I didn't listen to music. I liked it quiet.

Besides, I had to prepare myself for my interview with Skye Travels.

Skye Travels was an up and coming private airline. I didn't remember it from when I lived in Houston ten years ago, but I hadn't been focused on the world of aviation at the time. In addition to my course work, my activities in the ROTC Silver Wings program had kept every minute of my days more than occupied.

Until I'd taken those two weeks off at the end of my last semester and before I reported to duty.

According to my quick dive on the Internet, Skye Travels had cornered the market on private airlines in Houston.

They also had planes scattered all across the country. Dallas. Mackinac Island. Denver. From what I'd read, Noah Worthington even started the company in Dallas. I was curious about the history of the company, but that would probably require asking someone who worked there. Maybe even Noah Worthington himself.

The wheels touched down in a remarkably smooth landing as the pilot switched to reverse thrust.

The cabin shook and people silently braced themselves.

I sat quietly, mentally going through the motions involved in bringing a plane to the ground, then taxing along the tarmac.

For most passengers, the flight was over. But I knew how much work the pilots still had to do before the doors opened.

I had no reason to be nervous. I was a seasoned air force pilot who'd logged an enormous number of flight hours.

But not in the civilian world.

There was a chance that Noah wouldn't hire me for that reason. It took a different skill set to fly passengers from point A to point B while catering to their whims than it did to fly a fighter jet.

I was the daughter of a full bird colonel—retired, so I hadn't grown up anywhere in particular. But I'd spent five college years in Houston... the longest I'd lived anywhere. So that made me think of Houston as home.

I didn't know anyone here. I wasn't the kind of girl who had girlfriends. I had work friends, but they changed regularly along with my location.

If I didn't get this job with Skye Travels, I would have to pick somewhere else to apply. It probably hadn't been smart to put all my eggs in one basket, especially since I didn't have a backup plan. No clue where else I would want to live other than Houston.

It wasn't like I needed a job—not for money. I was getting full Air Force retirement. But the thought of having endless days with no purpose gave me hives.

I needed to work and since flying was my life, it made sense that I would apply to work as a pilot. I didn't have the certifications to apply for commercial jobs. That was okay. I honestly didn't think a commercial job would keep me busy enough.

The plane came to a stop and ninety percent of the passengers jumped out of their seats. It wasn't like they could anywhere until it was time.

I sat calmly in my seat and waited. The flight wasn't over until the doors opened and it was my turn to exit the plane.

All those people standing impatiently did nothing to speed things along.

I pulled out my phone and switched it from airplane mode.

With retirement, even at thirty-four, my phone had gone noticeably quiet. Not having any responsibilities meant not having any messages or calls. I not had no friends, but other than my parents, I had no family. My parents stayed in Germany while my father retired. We'd never been close, and now, with them living halfway across the world, we had even less need to stay in touch with each other.

I had nothing against them. They did their thing and I did my thing. With both my father and me being military, our schedules rarely allowed for family time.

That might change now that we were both retired.

Retired. Such an odd word for me to be using to describe myself.

If I had anything to do with it, my so-called retirement was going to last about half a minute.

All I had to do was to convince Noah Worthington to hire me to fly for him.

Then I could settle in to a job that would keep my sufficiently busy in the city that held my fondest memories.

It wasn't too much to ask. A meaningful job. A place to call home.

Quinn Worthington

Buried beneath paperwork again.

Soothing classic music spilled out of the phone sitting on my desk and beneath the music was another layer—the heavy sound of jets coming and going.

I gave my eyes a rest and picked up my cup of coffee, almost too cold to drink.

As the youngest of five children to airline mogul Noah Worthington, I'd found my way to the position of Vice-President of Skye Travels.

My father, Noah Worthington, was of course, president and would be until the moment he died. I was content to be vice-president, but I wanted more out of the position than merely being a paper-pusher. I was making progress in adding PR to my position.

At thirty-five, I already had more responsibility than most people my age. Despite what people liked to assume—since I was the owner's son—I'd worked my way up from the bottom.

As far as I was concerned, it was a good use of my business degree.

Anytime I thought it might not be challenging enough, all I had to was to wait a minute for Noah to give me some new and challenging task.

Unfortunately, most those tasks involved paper in some way or another.

Despite cutting my teeth in the air, I'd never had a desire to be a pilot. Learning about engines and aerodynamics and everything aviation had never captured my passion.

I liked business. So no matter my complaints, I loved my job.

I pushed back in my chair and looked out over the tarmac. They only person who had a better view was my father. But I could see everything I needed to see. I didn't need to see the highway, too, from the corner office.

The tarmac was just fine. And on days like today I knew I had at least a little bit of my father in me.

It was Friday afternoon on a crisp October day. I watched in wonder as one of the big commercial jets lifted itself off the ground. I didn't need to know the hows and whys to find it fascinating.

Skye Travels had their own area at a corner of the airport.

We shared it with other private planes, but for all intents and purposes, we claimed it.

Noah was interviewing a pilot today. I didn't know who. It didn't matter to me until he signed them up. Then I went to work. It was my job to teach them how to use the computer program where everything happened from flights to paydays. If they didn't learn to use the system, they didn't get paid.

For some reason, pilots found it challenging. For me, it was simple.

My father strode out the back door toward the Cessna Citation sitting outside the hangar. The bright red Skye Travels logo was splashed across the tail.

My father was an eccentric man. He could afford to be. He'd taken an idea and nurtured it into a thriving business. A man to be envied to be sure.

His eccentricity manifested itself primary in his relationships with his pilots.

He'd been known to open satellite services in states in order to keep pilots with the company. He had two pilots based out of Mackinac Island right now.

Every time Father did these things, he just added another layer of wealth to his empire. And another layer of paperwork to my job.

Father also had interesting ways of interviewing pilots. A way that made the businessman in me cringe. As his son, I just shrugged it off. It seemed to work. Noah only hired the best.

Sometimes he just met with them and had a friendly conversation about nothing in particular in his office.

Sometimes he had them fly for him.

Either way, I was pretty sure he knew who he was going to hire before he ever laid eyes on them.

Father reached the airplane and opened the door. It looked like today was going to be one of those times when the interviewee got to pilot a plane for him.

Interesting. Sometimes I'd like to be inside my father's head to see just how he made his business decisions.

After hiring pilots, Father often brought them to our weekly family dinners, often with interesting ramifications. Two of my four sisters had married pilots Father had introduced them to.

We'd had a couple of female pilots working for us over the years. Father never brought them home. It made me wonder if he didn't introduce my sisters to certain pilots on purpose.

I wouldn't put it past him.

At any rate, the fact that he never brought the female pilots around led me to believe that he respected my wishes.

I didn't date and I'd made that clear to my family.

It wasn't that I didn't like women.

On the contrary.

It was just that there was one particular girl who had stolen my heart.

It had been a ridiculously long time ago... ten years, but I had not changed my mind.

She was the girl I was going to marry.

All I had to do was to find her again.

Keep reading Second Chance Destiny...

Kathryn Kaleigh is the author of over seventy novels, over one hundred short stories, and many collections.

kathrynkaleigh.com